"Son

Something about th...
the back of her neck shiver. She ~~d~~...
before. But where…

The breath she had just inhaled backed up in her lungs. Oh no, it *couldn't* be.

She glanced up at him out of the corner of her eye as he approached the table...and swiftly looked away, heart pounding. He had the same smoldering black eyes, the solid, square jaw, the full lips that had kissed her senseless. But it couldn't be him. Could it? Her mind must be playing tricks on her.

She had a strict rule of never sleeping with a coworker. Especially one she would be working with directly. And definitely not one whose work she would be putting under the microscope.

"Rob," Demitrio said. "This is Caroline Taylor. Caroline, this is my son, Rob, our director of marketing."

She had no choice but to look up, to meet his eyes.…

Dear Reader,

Life, I have learned, is very short.

Keep the ones you love close,

Leave the past where it belongs,

Forgive or seek forgiveness,

Be happy.

Michelle

MICHELLE CELMER

CAROSELLI'S BABY CHASE

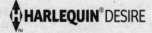

Recycling programs
for this product may
not exist in your area.

ISBN-13: 978-0-373-73239-5

CAROSELLI'S BABY CHASE

Printed in U.S.A.

Books by Michelle Celmer

Harlequin Desire

*Exposed: Her Undercover
  Millionaire* #2084
†*One Month with the Magnate* #2099
†*A Clandestine Corporate Affair* #2106
†*Much More Than a Mistress* #2111
The Nanny Bombshell #2133
Princess in the Making #2175
§*Caroselli's Christmas Baby* #2194
Bedroom Diplomacy #2210
§*Caroselli's Baby Chase* #2226

Silhouette Desire

The Secretary's Secret #1774
Best Man's Conquest #1799
*The King's Convenient Bride #1876
*The Illegitimate Prince's Baby #1877
*An Affair with the Princess #1900
*The Duke's Boardroom Affair #1919
Royal Seducer #1951
The Oilman's Baby Bargain #1970
*Christmas with the Prince #1979
Money Man's Fiancée Negotiation #2006
*Virgin Princess, Tycoon's Temptation #2026
*Expectant Princess, Unexpected Affair #2032
†*The Tycoon's Paternity Agenda* #2053

Harlequin Superromance

Nanny Next Door #1685

Harlequin Special Edition

No Ordinary Joe #2196

Silhouette Special Edition

Accidentally Expecting #1847

†Black Gold Billionaires
*Royal Seductions
§The Caroselli Inheritance

Other titles by this author
available in ebook format.

MICHELLE CELMER

is a bestselling author of more than thirty books. When she's not writing, she likes to spend time with her husband, kids, grandchildren and a menagerie of animals.

Michelle loves to hear from readers. Visit her website, www.michellecelmer.com, like her on Facebook or write her at P.O. Box 300, Clawson, MI 48017.

In memory of my nephew Devon,
who in seventeen years touched more lives
than most people manage in a lifetime

Prologue

Once a year since her death, on the day of her birth, December thirtieth, Giuseppe Caroselli honored Angelica, his wife of sixty-eight years and mother of his three sons, by making her favorite cake, raspberry walnut torte with dark chocolate frosting.

Caroselli chocolate, of course.

In less than an hour his family would be there to celebrate with him. To pass photos and share memories. On his request, his grandsons Rob and Tony had arrived early. They each sat on a barstool at the kitchen island, watching him carefully measure the ingredients and mix them together, the way they had when they were boys.

From birth, his three grandsons—Robert, Anthony Jr. and Nicholas—had been groomed to someday take over Caroselli Chocolate, the business Giuseppe had built from the ground up, after emigrating from Italy.

What he hadn't counted on was their being so resistant

to carrying on the Caroselli name. And if they didn't settle down and have sons of their own, the Carosellis would be no more. At least Nicholas now had the marriage part taken care of.

"As I'm sure you already know, Nicholas has forfeited his portion of the thirty-million dollars."

"He told us," Tony said, a perpetual frown on his face. So serious, that one. He needed to learn to take life in stride. Have fun.

"That means fifteen million each to you boys if you marry and produce a male heir," he told them.

"That's a lot of money," Rob said. He was the most driven of the three, the one who would no doubt take his father Demitrio's place as CEO one day. If Demitrio would only put aside his doubts and trust his son.

"It is a lot of money," Giuseppe agreed. Money that he had no intention of actually giving them. What sort of man would he be if he singled out only two of his seven grandchildren? And as he had suspected, Nick was so happy to be married, so content with his life, he had turned down his share.

One down, two to go.

And Giuseppe didn't doubt that like their cousin, in the end, Tony and Rob would make the right decision and do him proud.

In fact, he was counting on it.

One

As he watched his date leave the hotel bar wrapped around another man, Robert Caroselli wanted to feel angry or put out, or even mildly annoyed, but he couldn't work up the steam. He hadn't wanted to come to this party, but he'd let Olivia, a woman he'd been seeing casually, talk him into it last minute.

"I don't really feel like celebrating," he'd told her when she called him around nine. He had already turned off the television and was planning to crawl into bed and with any luck sleep away the next three months or so. It was that or face daily the fact that his family, the owners of Caroselli Chocolate, had lost complete faith in him as a marketing director.

Yes, sales for the last quarter were down, but they were in a recession for Christ's sake. Hiring Caroline Taylor, a so-called marketing genius from Los Angeles, was not only an insult, but also total overkill as far as he was concerned. But against the entire family, his objections carried little weight.

On top of that he had the added pressure of finding a wife. A woman to give him a male heir. By thirty-one most of his cousins, and the majority of his college buddies, were already married. It wasn't as if he'd made a conscious decision to stay single. His dedication to the family business had kept him too busy to settle down. He couldn't deny that ten-million dollars had been a tempting incentive, but fifteen million? That was difficult to pass up. Especially when it meant that if he didn't get his cut, his cousin Tony would walk away with the entire thirty million. He would never hear the end of it.

But if he was going to find a woman to be his wife and bear his children, it wouldn't be in a bar. And it definitely wouldn't be Olivia. Which was why he'd planned to stay home.

"You *can't* stay home alone on New Year's Eve!" Olivia had said. "Who will you kiss? You can't start the New Year without a kiss at midnight. It's…un-American!"

She hadn't seemed too concerned with whom he would kiss when she walked out the door with someone else. Not that he blamed her for bailing on him. He hadn't exactly been the life of the party. When they arrived around ten, he scoped out a counter-height table with two vacant barstools near the back corner, claimed it and hadn't moved since. Now he was on his—he counted the empty glasses in front of him—third Scotch and feeling a hell of a lot more relaxed than when he got there.

Alcohol flowed freely at every Caroselli family function—hell, his family would use any excuse to get together, drink and gossip—but Rob rarely indulged. He never much cared for the out-of-control feeling that came with intoxication. Tonight was a rare exception.

From his table he had a decent view of the entire bar, which was crammed above capacity with people, who, from his vantage point, undulated like the waves off the shore of Lake Michigan. Or maybe that was the liquor playing tricks with his vision.

"Excuse me!"

At the sudden shout, Rob jerked to attention. He blinked, then blinked again, positive he was imagining the angel who stood beside his table. A halo of pale blond hair hung in loose curls that nearly brushed her narrow waist, and framed a heart-shaped face that glowed with youth and good health. His gaze slipped lower and he realized that this particular angel had a body made for sin. She couldn't have been more than a few inches over five-feet tall, but she packed one hell of a figure into her skinny jeans and clingy blue sweater. A complete contrast to the wholesome beauty of her face.

"Is this seat taken?" she shouted over the music. "And just to be clear, I am *not* hitting on you. I've been on my feet all day and there isn't a single other free seat in this entire place."

He gestured to the chair across from his. "Help yourself."

"Thank you." She slid onto the stool, sighing with pleasure as her feet left the floor. "You're a lifesaver."

"No problem."

She offered him one fine-boned hand with short, neatly filed nails. "Carrie—"

Her last name was drowned out by the blare of a noisemaker. She shook his hand, her grip surprisingly firm for someone so petite and delicate-looking.

"Hi, Carrie, I'm Rob."

"Nice to meet you, Ron," she said.

He opened his mouth to correct her, but she flashed him

a smile so easy and sweet, so disarming, she could call him anything she wanted and it wouldn't have mattered to him. "Can I buy you a drink?"

She cocked her head to one side and smiled. "Are *you* hitting on *me?*"

He had never been the type to flirt, but he heard himself saying, "Would it be a problem if I was?"

She leaned forward to study him and his gaze was naturally drawn to the deep cleft at the front of her low-cut sweater. "I guess that just depends."

"On what?"

"Why a man like you would be sitting here alone at eleven-fifteen on New Year's Eve."

"A man like me?"

She rolled her eyes. "Don't even try to pretend that you don't know how hot you are. You should have women crawling all over you."

"I'm alone because my date left with someone else."

She blinked. "Was she blind or just stupid?"

He laughed. "Bored, I think. I'm not in a mood to celebrate."

Although the night was definitely looking up.

"You must have a girlfriend," she said.

He shook his head.

"Wife?"

He held up his ringless left hand.

She paused, then asked, "Gay?"

He laughed again. "Straight as an arrow."

"Hmm," she said, looking puzzled. "Are you a jerk?"

She sure didn't pull any punches. He liked a woman who was direct and to the point. "I'd like to believe I'm not, but I suppose everyone has their moments."

She nodded thoughtfully. "Honesty...I like that. My answer is yes. You can buy me a drink."

"What would you like?"

She nodded to his glass. "Whatever you're having."

He looked around, but the waitresses in the vicinity were overwhelmed with customers, so he figured it would be quicker to go right to the source. "Be right back," he said, heading for the bar.

It took several minutes to navigate through the crowd, and another five or ten before the bartender served him. As he walked back to the table, he half expected Carrie to be gone. He was pleasantly surprised to find her sitting there waiting for him, and suddenly grateful that he wouldn't have to watch the ball drop alone. He might even get a New Year's kiss out of it. Or maybe that would be pushing his luck. Maybe just a quick one, or if she wasn't into kissing a total stranger, a peck on the cheek even.

"Here you go." He set her drink in front of her and re-claimed his chair.

"That took so long, I started to think you left," she said.

"And I wasn't sure if you would still be here when I got back."

"I'm not blind or stupid," she said with a grin, and he felt a tug of attraction so intense, he nearly reached across the table for her hand.

"Do you live in the area?" she asked, sipping her drink.

"Lincoln Park."

"Is that far from here?"

"Not too far. I take it you're not from Chicago."

"West Coast born and bred. I'm here for work. I'm stay-ing in the hotel. That's how I wound up in this particu-lar bar."

"You must have someone back home."

"Not for a while."

"Are the men there blind or just stupid?"

She smiled, and he felt that tug again, only this time

it was lower, and it wasn't her hand he wanted to touch. That New Year's kiss was sounding even more appealing. He would have to call Olivia tomorrow and thank her for dragging him out.

"A lot of men feel threatened by a strong, successful woman," she said.

Rob had quite a few strong, successful women in his family, and compared to them, Carrie looked anything but threatening. His first instinct, when she had approached his table, was to pick her up and hug her.

"I also have the tendency to gravitate toward men who are bad for me," she said.

"Bad for you how?"

"I like jerks. It's my way of sabotaging the relationship before it even begins." She sipped her drink. "I have intimacy issues."

"If you know that, then why don't you date someone different?"

"Knowing what the problem is doesn't necessarily make it any easier to fix."

Well, she had the honesty thing down to a science. The women he met typically played up their good qualities, not their faults. Which he couldn't deny was, in an odd way, a refreshing change of pace. A sort of "this is me, take it or leave it" philosophy.

"When was your last serious relationship?" he asked.

"I've never really had one."

"Really? What are you? Twenty-four? Twenty-five?"

Carrie laughed. "Aren't you good for my ego. I'm twenty-eight."

"I've never met a woman past the age of eighteen who hasn't been in at least one serious relationship."

"Which you clearly find fascinating," she said, looking amused.

"I do." In more ways than just that. She was like the perfect woman. Sexy, desirable, with a decent sense of humor and completely uninterested in a relationship. Had he hit the jackpot or what?

"How about you?" Carrie asked. "Ever been in a serious relationship?"

"Engaged, but that was a long time ago. Back in college."

"What happened?"

"You could say that we wanted different things."

"What did you want?"

He shrugged. "Marriage, kids, the usual stuff."

"What did she want?"

"My roommate, Evan."

She winced. "Ouch."

"Better I found out what she was like before we were married than after. At that point I decided to focus on my career."

"So you're married to your job?"

"More or less."

"It's not unusual for me to work fourteen-hour days, so I totally get that."

She would be the first woman who ever did. And he found himself wishing she were staying in Chicago longer than a few days. She was someone he wouldn't mind getting to know better.

After talking for a few minutes more, and some serious flirting, they had both drained their glasses, so he hailed a waitress for two more drinks. There was more talking, more flirting—but mostly flirting—then Carrie had a third drink, and by then it was nearly midnight. At one minute till, the music stopped, and everyone focused on the big-screen television over the bar to watch the ball drop.

"So," Carrie said, "because neither of us has anyone to kiss…"

"I was told that it's un-American to start the New Year off without a kiss," he said.

"I guess that doesn't leave us much choice, then."

With a grin, he held out his hand and she took it. She slid down off the stool, and didn't show a bit of resistance as he tugged her closer. He should have been watching the ball drop, but he couldn't seem to peel his eyes away from her face. Standing this close he would have expected to see at least an imperfection or two, but her skin was flawless, her eyes such a clear gray they appeared bottomless. His eyes dropped to her mouth, to lips that looked full and soft and kissable.

Only an hour ago he had been dreading the arrival of the New Year, now he could hardly wait for those last thirty seconds to pass. Then it was twenty seconds, and when it reached ten, everyone in the bar started to count. Except for him and Carrie. Their eyes locked, and they stood so close now that her warm breath feathered against his lips. They waited in anticipation. Five…four…three…two…

Unable to wait another second, he slanted his mouth over hers and the cheers and hoots, the shrill of noisemakers and the chorus of "Auld Lang Syne" being sung—it all faded into the background. Her lips parted under his. He heard her sigh as he sank his fingers through the silky ribbons of her hair, felt her melt against him when he pulled her closer. The softness of her lips, the sweet taste of her mouth, were more intoxicating than any drink. And he wanted her, knew he had to have her, even if it was for only one night.

He wasn't sure how long they stood there kissing, their arms wrapped around one another, but when he finally broke the kiss, they were both breathless and Carrie's cheeks were rosy and hot.

"At the risk of sounding too forward," she said, "would you like to come up to my room?"

Of course he wanted to. "Are you sure that's what you want?"

That must have been the right answer, because she smiled and took his hand. "I am now. I figure, why not start the year with a *bang?*"

He grinned, squeezed her hand and said, "Let's go."

Two

Start the year off with a bang indeed, Carrie thought as the cab inched along in bumper-to-bumper traffic through the slushy streets of Chicago. Two days later and her neck still ached, there was a bruise on her shin where she had banged it on the headboard, and she had angry-looking rug burns on her knees, but it had been *so* worth it. She hadn't been *banged* so well, or so many times in a row, in years. The man was insatiable, and gave as good as he got. Better even. And as she had imagined, he looked just as good out of his clothes as he did in them. She would even go so far as to say that it was the single most satisfying, fun and adventurous sexual experience of her life. Then he had to go and ruin it by skulking off in the middle of the night without even saying goodbye.

He hadn't left his phone number, which she could have looked up if she had caught his last name. But all evidence pointed to his not wanting to be found. For all she knew,

Ron wasn't even his real name, and he had been sitting there alone looking for someone just like her, someone to *bang* in the New Year with. Maybe all he'd really wanted was cheap sex.

Oh, well. At least it had been really *good* cheap sex. And in her own defense, she'd hit the minibar in her room before she had even ventured downstairs and had been more than a little drunk. It was possible that he wasn't even as good-looking as she thought. Or that great of a lover.

She wasn't sure if that should make her feel better or worse.

She had been in Chicago barely forty-eight hours, and already she'd invited a strange man up to her room, had sex and had gotten dumped. That had to be some kind of world record.

But Ron—if that was really his name—wasn't totally to blame. She did have the tendency to come on a little strong, and sometimes men took it the wrong way. Under normal circumstances she was outspoken. Get her a little tipsy and she had the tendency to say things she probably shouldn't. According to her stepfather, her sassy mouth had been her biggest problem. And his cure for that had always been a solid crack across said mouth with the back of his hand.

She didn't recall everything she and Ron had discussed that night, but she seemed to remember some of it being very personal in nature.

"This is it," the cab driver said as the car rolled to a stop outside Caroselli Chocolate headquarters. As soon as the contracts were signed, and a timetable set, she would look for an apartment or condo to lease. There was nothing she hated more than living out of suitcases for extended periods of time.

She paid him, grabbed her briefcase, climbed out of the cab and walked to the revolving front door, the damp cold seeping through her coat, the heels of her pumps clicking against the slushy pavement. She pushed her way inside, into a lobby of glass, stainless steel and marble, and walked to the guard station, the alluring scent of chocolate drawing her gaze to the gift shop at the other end of the lobby.

"Caroline Taylor. I'm here for a meeting," she told the guard.

"Good morning, Ms. Taylor. They're expecting you." He handed her a name badge that said "Guest," which she clipped to the lapel of her suit jacket. "Take the elevator behind me up to the third floor and see the receptionist."

"Thank you." She walked to the elevator, back straight, head high. There was no lack of security cameras, and it was critical to make a good impression the second she walked in the door. Despite her reputation, and her impeccable record for getting the job done, some people, men of a certain era in particular, sometimes doubted her abilities. And this being a family business, she had no doubt that she would be working with several generations of Carosellis.

As she rode up to the third floor she shrugged out of her overcoat and draped it over her arm. When the doors slid open she stepped out of the elevator into another reception area. A young woman whose nameplate announced her as Sheila Price was seated behind a large desk, and beside her stood an attractive, older gentleman in a very expensive, exquisitely tailored suit. Considering his age, and the air of authority he exuded, she was guessing he was one of the three Caroselli brothers, the sons of Giuseppe who now ran the company.

She walked to the desk, nervous energy propelling her steps. She hadn't planned to expand her business outside the West Coast area for another year or two, but Caroselli Chocolate was the largest and most prestigious company to approach her thus far, and when they called, it was too good an opportunity to pass up. Of course, if she botched it up, it would decimate her reputation and probably destroy her career.

But that wasn't going to happen.

"Welcome, Ms. Taylor," the man said, stepping forward to greet her. "I'm Demitrio Caroselli."

"It's a pleasure," she said, shaking his hand, a little surprised that the CEO himself was there to greet her.

"Can I take your coat?" Sheila asked.

"Yes, thank you," she said, handing it over.

"Everyone is waiting for us in the conference room," Demitrio said, gesturing down a long hallway lined with offices. "It's this way."

Being a private contractor, Carrie answered to no one, and being in such high demand, she walked into every meeting knowing she had the upper hand. That didn't mean she wasn't slightly nervous. But she seriously doubted they would have shelled out the expense of a first-class plane ticket and a five-star hotel if they weren't seriously planning to sign the contract.

"Do you prefer Caroline or Ms. Taylor?" he asked.

"Caroline or Carrie," she told him.

"We appreciate your coming to see us on such short notice," he said. "And so close to the holidays."

"I'm happy to be here." The assignment back in L.A. that she was supposed to have started this week had been cancelled when the company went under last month; otherwise she wouldn't have been available until much later this year.

"Is this your first visit to Chicago?"

"It is. From what I've seen it's a beautiful city. The snow will take some getting used to, though." The hall was silent and most of the offices they passed were dark. "Is it always this quiet?"

"We're not technically back from the holiday break until next Monday," he said. "The holiday season is a very busy time for us so we give everyone the first week of the year off."

At the end of the hall he opened a door marked "Conference Room" and Carrie held her breath as they stepped inside. In front of a bank of windows that spanned the entire length of the room stood a strikingly beautiful young woman who looked more suited to a fashion runway than a company boardroom. On one side of a marble-topped table long enough to seat a dozen-plus people sat two dashing older men and opposite them, two younger men, who frankly buried the needle on the totally hot-and-sexy scale.

Well, *damn,* the Caroselli family sure did grow them tall dark and sexy.

She assumed one of them was Robert Caroselli, the man whose department she was there to analyze and pick apart. In her experience, that didn't typically go over very well, and resulted in a certain degree of opposition. Especially when the person in charge was a man.

"Caroline," Demitrio said, "these are my brothers Leo, our CFO, and Tony, our COO."

The two older men rose to shake her hand. Tony was shorter and stockier in build. Leo was the tallest of the three and very fit for a man his age. Despite their physical differences, there was no mistaking the fact that they were related.

"Nice to meet you, gentlemen."

"And this is my niece, Elana. She heads up our accounting division."

Elana sauntered over to shake Carrie's hand. Her firm grip was all business, her smile cool and sophisticated, but her dark eyes were warm and friendly. Carrie was fairly adept at reading people, and if she had to guess, she would say that Elana was incredibly intelligent, though underestimated at times because of her beauty.

"On this side we have my nephew, Nick," Demitrio said. "He's the genius behind our new projects."

Nick, the one on the left, rose to shake her hand. He was charmingly attractive in a slightly rumpled I'm-sexy-and-rich-therefore-I-can-wear-a-wrinkled-shirt sort of way. The twinkle in his dark eyes, and slightly lopsided grin as he shook her hand said he was a flirt, while the wedding band on his left hand said he was very likely a harmless one.

"And last but not least," Demitrio said, while Carrie braced herself, "this is Tony Jr., director of overseas production and sales."

What about Robert?

Tony Jr. stood so tall that even in three-inch heels Carrie had to crane her neck to meet his eyes. His professional nod and distracted smile said that he had something other than the business at hand on his mind.

"Please have a seat," Demitrio said, gesturing to the empty chair beside Nick. "We're waiting for one more, then we can get started."

She'd barely settled in her seat when behind her she heard the door open, and a deep voice say, "Sorry I'm late. My secretary isn't back today, so I had to pick these reports up on my way in."

Something about that voice made the hair on the back of her neck shiver to attention. She'd definitely heard it before. But where…

The breath she had just inhaled backed up in her lungs. Oh no, it *couldn't* be.

She glanced up at him out of the corner of her eye as he approached the table, his attention on the pile of folders he carried, and when she focused on his face…

She swiftly looked away, heart pounding. He had the

same smoldering black eyes, the solid, square jaw, the full lips that had kissed her senseless. At first glance the resemblance was uncanny. But it couldn't be him. Could it?

He mumbled an "excuse me" as he laid a folder in front of her. On his right hand was a college ring identical to the one she had seen the other night, and as the scent of his aftershave drifted her way, the wave of familiarity was so strong that her heart skipped a beat.

She stared at the folder cover, unable to focus. Hell, she could barely *breathe*.

It's not him, she assured herself. *It just looks like him, and smells like him, and* sounds *like him...and wears the same ring as him.* But it *had* to be a coincidence, her mind playing tricks on her.

She had a strict rule of never sleeping with a coworker. Especially one she would be working with directly. And definitely not one whose work she would be putting under the microscope. She'd made that mistake once before, on her first high-profile job with a previous client. Previous because the affair had ended in disaster, the aftermath ugly.

It wasn't necessary for the entire team to like her, but maintaining their respect was crucial. When she recalled the things she and Ron had said to one another, the things she let him do...the sheer mortification made her want to curl inside her own skin and hide, or slide down out of her chair under the table.

As he rounded the table she kept her eyes on the folder, pretending to read, afraid to lift her head. Maybe if it was Ron, he wouldn't recognize her. They had both been pretty drunk.

"Rob," Demitrio said, "this is Caroline Taylor. Caroline, this is my son Rob, our director of marketing."

She had no choice but to look up, to meet his eyes, and when she did, her head spun and her heart sank.

Unless "Rob" had an identical twin, he was in fact Ron, her New Year's bang.

Rob blinked, then blinked again. In the conservative suit that hid her pinup model figure, with her granny hairstyle, he almost didn't recognize Carrie. But the slightly too-large clear gray eyes were a dead giveaway.

She sat frozen, watching him expectantly, and his first thought was that this had to be some sort of prank. Were Nick and Tony screwing with him? He'd bragged to them about the blonde beauty he'd spent the night with. Which his cousins knew was completely out of character for him. He didn't do drunken one-night stands. Typically, he didn't do drunken *anything*.

Was this some twisted practical joke? Had they gone to the hotel to look for her, maybe paid her to pose as Caroline Taylor to mess with Rob's head?

He looked from Nick to Tony, waiting for someone to say something, for everyone at the table to burst out laughing. And when they didn't, when they all watched him, looking increasingly puzzled by his lack of a response, he began to get a *very* bad feeling.

"Rob?" his dad said, brow creased with concern. "Is everything all right?"

"Fine," he said, a bit too enthusiastically, and forcing a smile that felt molded from plastic, he told Ms. Taylor, "It's a pleasure to meet you."

Not.

When he'd slipped out of her bed, he'd had no intention of ever seeing her again. Talk about dumb freaking luck.

Caroline nodded in his general direction, her head held a little too high, her shoulders too square and her back too straight, as if she'd been cut out of cardboard and propped up in the chair. She was clearly no happier to see him than he was to see her.

"Well, why don't we get started," his dad said, and everyone opened their folders. Rob tried to concentrate as they went over the contracts, and discussed Ms. Taylor's credentials and her projected time line, but he found his mind—and his eyes—wandering to the woman across the table. She downplayed her looks for work, he assumed in an attempt to gain respect from men who might otherwise objectify her or see her as too pretty to be smart. But he knew what she was hiding under that shapeless suit. The siren's figure and satin-soft skin. He knew the way her hair looked cascading down her bare back in silky ribbons, pale and buttery against her milky complexion, and how it brushed his chest as she straddled him. Even though parts of that night were a bit fuzzy, he knew he could never erase from his mind the image of her lying beneath him, wrapped in his arms, her breathy moans as he—

"Rob?" his dad said.

Rob jerked to attention. "Yeah, sorry."

"It seems we've covered everything."

Already?

"Why don't you take Caroline on a tour of the building while the rest of us have a short discussion. I'll call you when we're ready."

They had covered everything, and he hadn't heard a word of it. Now they would make the final decision, and they were going to do it without him. He'd been clear from day one that he considered her presence there a waste of time and money, and he had never once swayed from that opinion. Still it was a slap in the face to be excluded, not just for him, but for the entire marketing staff that he represented.

Or maybe, getting her alone for a few minutes wasn't such a bad idea. And meeting her wasn't "dumb luck" after all. Maybe a little time alone would give him the opportunity to make her see reason. See that she didn't belong here. Then she would no longer be his problem.

With a smile—a genuine one this time—he rose from his seat and said, "If you'll follow me, Ms. Taylor."

She stood, spine straight, shoulders back, flashing the others a confident smile, as if she already knew she had it in the bag. "I look forward to your decision."

Rob held the door for her, then followed her out, closing it firmly behind him. He turned to her and said in a low voice, "I think we need to talk."

Her eyes shooting daggers, her voice dripping with venom, she said, "Oh, you think so...*Ron?*"

He gestured down the hall. "My office is this way."

They walked there in silence, but he could feel her anger reverberating against the walls like an operatic vibrato.

His secretary's chair was unoccupied as they walked past, and when they were in his office he shut the door. He turned to face her and thought, *Here we go.* "I can see that you're upset."

"Upset," she said, her voice rising an octave. "Not only did you *lie* about your name, but did you have to skulk away in the middle of the night?"

If that's all she was mad about, he considered himself lucky. "First off, I did not lie to you about my name. I said it was Rob. You called me Ron and I saw no point in correcting you."

"I can't believe you didn't make the connection. Carrie Taylor, Caroline Taylor? You didn't at least suspect we might be one in the same person?"

"It was loud in the bar. I didn't even hear your last name. And we never discussed what we do for a living, so how was I supposed to guess who you were? I've met a lot of people named Carrie. You don't have a monopoly on the name."

"And as for skulking off in the middle of the night?"

"It was not the middle of the night. It was early morning and I didn't want to wake you. You were so drunk I'm not sure I could have if I tried. And I did not skulk. I got dressed and left, end of story."

"First off, I wasn't *that* drunk. And didn't it occur to you to at least leave a note?"

"Why would I? We agreed it would never be more than one night. It was over."

She rolled her eyes. "You know *nothing* about women do you? You could have said goodbye, told me that you had a good time."

"I assumed, in our case, actions spoke louder than words."

She didn't seem to have a snarky reply for that one. She couldn't deny it had been damned good for her, too.

"What I don't understand is why we're in here," Rob told her, "when you should be in the conference room telling them you can't work here."

Her brows rose. "Why would I do that?"

"Well, first, despite what my family believes, your services are not required or desired by anyone on my staff. And considering the circumstances, I don't think your presence here would be appropriate."

"What circumstances are those?"

Was she kidding? "The ones we've been discussing

since we stepped in here. It's unlikely either of us could be objective in light of what happened the other night."

"I don't know about you, but now that I know what a macho jerk you are, it isn't going to be an issue for me. In fact, I think I'm going to enjoy it."

He had been accused of being inattentive, arrogant and at times insufferable, but macho jerk was a new one. "Are you sure about that?"

"Absolutely."

"You can remain completely objective?"

"Yep."

Rob was not the type of man to behave rashly. He never made a move before he'd had time to completely think through a situation, weigh the pros and cons. So maybe it was pride that propelled him forward, or the satisfaction of proving her wrong, or just compromised judgment that motivated him to take her by the arms, pull her to him and crush his mouth down on hers.

Carrie made an indignant sound and pushed at his chest. She resisted for all of three seconds, then her fingers curled into the lapels of his jacket and her lips parted beneath his.

Having made his point, he should have let go. Instead he wrapped his arms around her, pulled her closer. It had been just like this on New Year's, his brain shutting down the second he kissed her, his body reacting on pure instinct, a carnal need to overpower and dominate. One that he'd never felt with a woman before her. Because despite her claim, he was not a macho jerk. Of all his cousins and uncles, he was probably the least chauvinistic man in the family. Her gender had no bearing whatsoever on his professional opinion.

Carrie slid her hands up his chest, tunneled them through his hair, taking two fistfuls and jerking his head back so she could kiss—*ow*—make that *bite* his neck.

Growling, he backed her against his office door, cringing as her head hit the surface with a *thunk,* cushioned only by the ugly bun in her hair, but it only seemed to fuel her desire.

"I want you right here, against this door," she said, her eyes locking on his as she slid her hand between their bodies, gripping his erection through his slacks.

Sucking in a breath, he grabbed the hem of her skirt and shoved his hand underneath, sliding it up her leg, and— damn—she was wearing a garter. He had just reached the top of her bare inner thigh, his fingers brushing the crotch of her panties, when his cell phone started to ring.

Damn it. Talk about lousy timing.

Carrie grumbled unhappily as he pulled his hand from under her skirt and backed away from the hand that had been busy unzipping his fly. "Yeah," he answered.

"We're ready for you," his father said.

"Be right there." He hung up without saying goodbye, so his dad wouldn't hear his labored breathing, and told Carrie, "They're ready for you."

She nodded, her cheeks rosy, pupils dilated. "I just need a minute to catch my breath."

He shoved his phone back in his pocket and zipped his pants. "Now do you see what I mean?"

"That you have pitiful lack of self-control?" Carrie said, straightening her jacket and smoothing the wrinkles from a skirt six inches too long for her height. "I definitely noticed that."

"I didn't see you trying to stop me."

She looked up at him, her lipstick kissed away, a stubborn tilt to her chin. "You enjoy being right, don't you?"

"Not always." Not this time. They had chemistry, but

that was about it. With fifteen million dollars riding on his choice, she was the exact opposite of what he was looking for in a woman. Not only did he consider her the enemy, but she'd said herself that she had intimacy issues, and she had never been in a serious relationship. Rob needed a woman with baby fever, someone to marry and pop out a male heir. She wasn't it, and having her around to tempt him would only make a difficult situation that much more tense.

"So, have I made my point?" he asked Carrie.

"You certainly have," she said. "We should get back to the conference room."

They walked side by side down the corridor, an uncomfortable silence building a wedge between them. There was nothing left to say. It had been fun, and now it was over. She would go back to California, and he and his team would work out a plan to beef up sales. And hopefully, sooner rather than later, he would find a woman to give him a son, and everyone would be happy.

The conference room was silent as they stepped inside. Carrie took her seat, and Rob returned to his.

"Sorry to make you wait," his dad told her.

"I completely understand," she said.

Rob waited for her to break the bad news, but she just sat there.

"After going over the final numbers," his uncle Leo said, "we're pleased to tell you that we agree to your terms and we would like you to start first thing next Monday morning."

Rob waited for the big letdown, wondered how everyone would take her turning down their offer.

"I don't come cheap," she said, then looked directly at Rob. "But I don't disappoint."

She may as well have drawn her sword and challenged him to a duel. And clearly she had only been humoring him. She had never intended to turn down the assignment.

If that was really the way she wanted to play this, fine.

You want a fight, sweetheart? Well, now you've got one.

Three

After the contracts were signed, everyone filed out of the conference room, shaking Carrie's hand, congratulating her and welcoming her to the company. Rob watched, gathering the binders—a task typically left for an assistant—growing increasingly impatient as Elana stopped to admire Carrie's briefcase of all things, and they launched into a conversation about women's purses and accessories. When he'd run out of ways to stall, he flat-out asked Elana, "Could I have a minute with Ms. Taylor?"

Flashing him a knowing look and a wry smile, Elana said, "Sure, Robby. See you Monday, Carrie."

Elana knew that there was no faster way to irritate him than to address him by his childhood nickname. The first half of it anyway. It had been years since anyone dare uttered the phrase that had been the bane of his existence from kindergarten to his first year of college.

She left, closing the door behind her, and Rob turned to Carrie, who was sliding papers into her briefcase.

"Well?" he said.

She closed the case and smiled up at him. "Something wrong...*Robby?*"

That was it—Elana was dead meat. "Why did you lie to me?"

She smiled, the picture of innocence. "When did I lie to you?"

"We agreed that in light of what happened, working together would be a bad idea."

"No, *you* said working together would be bad, and I commented on how you enjoy being right. I never said you *were* right."

"So you were just screwing with me?"

She propped her hands on the conference table, leaning in. "Not unlike the way *you* were screwing with *me*."

She definitely had him there. And he had best be going, before he told her what he really thought of her. "I'll see you Monday."

She smiled brightly. "Sure thing, Robby. Oh, and by the way, the first step will be analyzing your marketing data. I'll need a few things from you."

Gathering his patience, he said, "All right."

"I'll need all the data you have for the past twenty years."

He blinked. "*Twenty* years?"

"That's right."

He wondered if she really needed to go that far back, or if she was trying to make his life a living hell. Probably the latter, and could he blame her if she was? But that, she should realize, was a two-way street.

"It could take some time to compile everything. We've

been in the process of digitizing our older files. Some of it might still be in hard copy."

"That's fine. Just have it on my desk Monday morning."

"If you hadn't noticed, there's no one here. Everyone is on holiday vacation until Monday."

"Well," she said, the sweet smile not wavering a fraction. "Who better to do it than the director himself. Which reminds me, I'll need you available, and at my disposal at all times in case I have any questions."

Gritting his teeth, he nodded, then turned and walked to the door.

"Hey, Robby?"

Jaw tense, he turned back to her.

"I'm not the enemy. This will be as productive or as difficult as you make it. I think you'll find that I can be very pleasant to work with."

"So I noticed," he said, his eyes raking over her. "Will we be meeting for a quickie in my office daily, or just once or twice a week?" He didn't even like her, but his libido didn't seem to notice or care. It was telling him to rip that shapeless, ugly suit from her body, to pluck the pins from her granny hairstyle so he could watch her silky blond curls cascade down her shoulders.

She sighed and shook her head, as if she felt sorry for him. "Robby, is that the best you can do? You think I haven't heard worse? During the course of my career I've been called sweetie and sugar and pumpkin. I've been groped and fondled, objectified and demoralized. I've seen it all, and in the end I always get the job done, and I manage to do it with dignity."

She slung her case strap over her shoulder and said, "We can do this the easy way or the hard way. If you think you'd like to take me on, by all means give it your best shot. But

I should warn you, I always get what I want, and I'm not above fighting dirty."

He should have anticipated that. No one got as far as she had in the business world without being tough as nails. And shame on him for underestimating her.

She walked out, the heels of her shoes clicking as she marched down the hall. He had no plan to demoralize or objectify her, or to call her condescending names. And the only physical contact they might have would be totally at her discretion. He had every intention of treating her with the utmost respect, because he didn't doubt that she had earned it. His cooperation, however, was another matter altogether.

Rob walked to his office and sat down at his computer to send his staff and his secretary an email dictating what Carrie would need—one they would see Monday when they returned to work. He refused to make his people work a weekend they had been promised as vacation.

There was a knock on his door, and he looked up to see Tony and Nick standing there.

"Hey." He motioned them in, and Nick shut the door.

"So what was that all about?" Tony asked him.

"Yeah," Nick said, "what the heck did you say to her when you two left the conference room?"

"You probably wouldn't believe me if I told you." Rob could barely believe it himself. "Do you think my dad noticed?"

"Dude, *everyone* noticed," Nick said. "You looked as if either you wanted to kill each other, or tear each other's clothes off."

It was a little bit of both. "Remember the woman I told you about? The blonde from the bar?"

Tony nodded. "What about her?"

Nick being Nick, he was way ahead of Tony. He started to laugh. "No way. No one's luck could be *that* bad."

"Apparently it can."

Tony looked from Nick to Rob, and then he laughed. "Are you saying that Caroline Taylor is Carrie from the bar?"

He glared at them both. "I'm glad you find this so amusing."

"More ironic than amusing," Tony said.

"Yeah," Nick agreed. "But still funny as hell."

If it were happening to anyone but him, Rob probably would have thought so, too.

"So what are you going to do?" Tony asked.

"What can I do? I already asked her to leave, said it would be a conflict of interest for her to stay, and you can see how well that went."

"Did you see how much we're paying her?" Tony said. "Can you blame her for not walking away?"

"Well, I'm going to make sure that she earns every penny."

Tony shook his head, like he thought that was a bad idea. "You know that if you screw with her, your dad will be pissed."

"Not if he doesn't find out."

"You don't think she'll rat you out?" Nick asked.

"Only if she wants the entire family to know how she and I first met. If it gets around that she picks up men in bars for one-night stands, her credibility will be in the toilet. Every potential future client will believe that a bedroom romp is included in the contract."

"You don't think that's a little harsh?" Nick said.

If she could play dirty, so could he. "I'm not the one who declared war in front of the entire family. And you can damn well bet she plans to discredit me and my team every opportunity she gets."

"Are you sure? She comes off as smart and savvy but not vindictive."

If Nick had just heard her in the conference room, he might feel differently. And if she could be ruthless, so could Rob. She was on his turf now, and she would play by his rules.

"Nick and I are getting a late breakfast at the diner," Tony said. "Are you going to hang around and work, or do you want to come?"

He thought of all the work Carrie expected him to complete before Monday and smiled. "Breakfast sounds good."

He was getting ready to stand when his office phone rang. It was his sister Megan. "Give me fifteen minutes and I'll meet you by the elevator."

"We'll get our coats," Tony said.

"Hey, Meggie," he said. "What's up?"

"I just heard from the real estate agent," she said, her voice squeaky with excitement. "They accepted my offer! The apartment is mine!"

"Congratulations," Rob said. His younger sister had spent the past nine months looking for exactly the right place, and had been outbid on the first two. "And you're sure it's within your budget?"

"That's my other good news! You know Rose Gold-wyn?"

Rob had met her briefly at work, then a few times at family gatherings. She was a recent hire. The daughter of the woman who had been *Nonno's* secretary for the better part of his career.

Rose seemed nice enough, but there was something about her, something just a little…off. "What about her?" Rob said.

"She's going to be my roommate."

"But you hardly know her."

"Actually we've been talking a lot lately. We have a lot in common."

"Isn't she like twenty years older than you?"

"What difference does that make?"

"I don't know, Meg. Something about her…"

"What?"

"I don't trust her."

"Robby, I'm twenty-five" was her plucky response. "It's not your job to protect me anymore."

It would always be his job to protect her. She was an infant when his parents adopted her, and although he was six years older, they had always been close. He'd set her classmates straight when they made fun of her for looking "different" than the rest of her family. "Do me a favor and at least have legal do a background check on her. Just in case."

Her sigh of exasperation meant she was giving in. "Fine, if it makes you happy."

"It does." From the hallway he heard a door slam, then after a two- or three-second pause, raised voices. One of them definitely belonged to their father.

What the hell?

"Meggie, I have to go. I'll call you later."

"Love you, Robby!"

"Love you, too, Megs."

He got up and walked past his secretary's desk into the hall. At one end, near the conference room stood his dad and his uncle Tony, and his dad looked furious.

"I was never given a choice," his dad was saying, to which his uncle Tony answered, "You gave that up when you left her."

Whatever that meant, his dad's face flushed deep red

and he gave his brother a firm, two-handed shove that sent him stumbling backward several feet into the conference room door.

Rob had seen his dad and uncles argue, and at times it could get heated, but he had never seen them come to blows. Uncle Tony was stocky and muscular, but Demitrio, Rob's dad, was taller, younger and trained by the military to fight. That apparently wasn't going to stop Uncle Tony because he looked as if he were about to lunge.

From behind him, Rob heard his cousin Tony yell, "What the hell is going on?" and turned to see Nick and him running down the hall toward the older men. Rob followed them.

Both older men, red-faced and out of breath, jaws and fists clenched, stopped and turned to him.

"What the hell, Dad?" Tony said. "What is with the two of you lately?"

Demitrio turned to Tony Sr. "Why don't you tell him, Tony."

"I'd like to know, too," Rob said. The last time Uncle Tony had been to their house, Rob showed up to find his mom in tears. He wanted to know why.

"Boys, this is between me and my brother," Tony Sr. said. "There's no need to be concerned—"

"Dad!" Tony said. "You were two seconds from beating the crap out of each other."

"It wouldn't be the first time I beat the crap out of him," Demitrio said, glaring at his brother.

"When you were kids maybe," Rob said, "but you're in your *sixties*. You could have a heart attack."

"Did I miss the fun?"

Rob turned to see Leo, Nick's dad, walking toward them.

"They're fighting," Tony said, as if he still couldn't believe it. "*Physically* fighting."

"It's nothing to worry about, boys," Leo said, laughing heartily. "You wouldn't believe how many times I had to get between these two when we were kids. It's that middle-child curse, I guess." He stepped strategically between his brothers and gave each of them a slap on the back. "Come on, gentlemen, let's go in my office and settle this." He turned to Rob and his cousins. "You boys can head on out. I've got this."

Reluctantly the three cousins walked to the elevator.

"So what do you think that was about?" Tony asked him.

"I don't know," Rob said. "But it's been building for a while now. Things have been tense for a couple of months."

"Don't forget, Tony's mom was arguing with your dad at Thanksgiving," Nick told Rob. Sarah, Tony's mom, used to date Rob's dad before he joined the army. The fact that Tony Sr. married her shortly after he left had been a minor source of friction among the three of them over the years. Certainly, it was nothing they would come to blows over now, unless the dynamics of those relationships had changed....

"Tony, you don't think that your mom and my dad..."

"Honestly, Rob, I don't know what to think anymore. But things have seemed off with my parents, as well. I went to a New Year's party with them and they seemed...I don't know, out of sync, if that makes sense. They're typically very physically affectionate with each other, and I barely saw them touch."

"Maybe my dad can help them figure it out," Nick said.

"Is your dad still sleeping with your mom?" Rob asked him.

Nick made a face. "Yeah. It's bad enough knowing about it, but to actually see them...you know..." He shuddered involuntarily. "Talk about scarring a person for life."

"That'll teach you to barge into your mom's house without knocking," Tony told him.

"I think it's pretty cool that after being divorced for so long, they reconnected," Rob said.

"They do seem happy," Tony told Nick. "Maybe I shouldn't mention this, but they were at the New Year's party, too. They couldn't keep their hands off each other, and they disappeared long before the ball dropped."

"Regardless," Nick said, "I'll never get how two people who despised each other, and had a messy and uncivilized divorce that scarred all three of their children, could suddenly change their minds and hop in the sack."

"I'm sure that if they'd had a choice, they would have preferred to be happy the first time around," Tony said.

Nick shrugged. "Yeah, I guess. So long as I don't have to see my dad's bare ass again, they can be 'happy' all they want."

"So, breakfast?" Tony said.

They said goodbye to Sheila as they passed the reception desk, then rode the elevator down to the lobby. Dennis, the security guard, nodded as they walked past.

"Who are you betting on in the playoffs?" Nick asked him, walking backward to the door.

"Steelers-Lions," Dennis said. "And the Lions will take it."

"No way! The Lions haven't won a championship since what, the fifties?"

"Fifty-seven," Dennis said. "But this is the year."

Nick laughed. "Dream on. I say Steelers-Chargers, and the Steelers will take the championship."

Dennis grinned and shook his head. "Keep dreaming, boss."

Nick laughed as they walked out the door into the bitter wind. Parking was a bitch downtown, so they pulled up their collars and walked the three blocks to the restaurant. The pavement was slick, so it was slow-going, and by the time they got to the diner it was already filling up with the lunch crowd. Every seat was taken and there was a line of people ahead of them.

"Feel like waiting?" Tony asked.

Rob shrugged. "Could be a while."

"I say we wait," Nick said. "It's too damn cold to go back out there."

"Hey, Caroselli!" someone called. Rob followed the voice, cursing under his breath when he realized whom it belonged to.

Four

"Is that Carrie?" Nick asked.

"That's her," Rob said. She sat alone in a booth near the back, and she was waving them over. She was still wearing the ugly suit, but she'd lost the shapeless jacket. She'd let her hair down so it fell in soft waves over the shoulder of a rose-colored shirt made of some sort of stretchy nylon that clung to her curves.

Tony's mouth dropped open. "Holy hell. No wonder you picked her up. Look at her."

"Yeah," Nick said. "Her body is...wow."

Yes, it was, and as much as he didn't want to, Rob couldn't help but look. Just as he couldn't help it the other night either. In her clothes she was smokin' hot, but out of them she was a goddess. A work of art.

But that was where the attraction ended.

"Looks like she wants to share her table," Nick said.

"I'd rather wait for a table," Rob told him. She had ruined enough of his day.

"Stop being a baby and go," Tony said, giving him a shove from behind. "You're going to have to get used to being around her."

But not outside of a work scenario, Rob thought, grumbling to himself all the way to her booth. And while he could have turned and walked out, he refused to show defeat, to let her win. To drive him from a restaurant he'd eaten in weekly for the past ten years.

She smiled up at them as they approached. "Hello, gentlemen. I saw you walk up and thought rather than wait, you might like to share. I stood in line about twenty minutes myself."

"We'd love to join you," Nick said, flashing her his "Charming Nick" smile. He and Tony slid into the empty side of the booth, leaving Rob no choice but to slide in beside Carrie, which earned each of them a malevolent look.

The booths weren't exactly spacious, and with her briefcase on the seat next to the window, there was no hope of putting any real space between them. She was so close he could feel her body heat, and every time either of them moved, their shoulders or arms bumped.

This day was going from bad to worse.

He refused to acknowledge the scent of her perfume, or shampoo, or whatever it was that had driven him mad the other night, or the lusty urges he was feeling as her leg brushed against his. The desire to run his hand up the inside of her thigh again, until he reached the garter holding up her stockings, had him shifting restlessly in his seat.

"Are we a little antsy?" Carrie asked him, but thankfully, before he had to come up with a viable excuse, the waitress appeared.

"Hey, boys," she said, stopping at the table with a pot

of coffee and four beat-up plastic cups of iced water. What the place lacked in class, it made up for in good food and quality service. "What can I getcha?"

Without even looking at the menu, they all ordered their usual breakfast, and after reviewing the menu, Carrie ordered the special, which was a lot of food for a woman her size.

"I take it you gentlemen come here often," Carrie said, reaching across the table for a coffee creamer, her shoulder bumping against Rob's.

"Best greasy spoon in the greater Chicago area," Tony said. "How did you stumble across it?"

"On my way out I asked Dennis where I could get a decent breakfast." She added a packet of artificial sweetener to her cup. "He told me to come here."

If Dennis wasn't such an exemplary employee, Rob might have considered that grounds for termination.

"So what do you think of Chicago?" Nick asked her.

"It's very cold. And windy."

"They call it the Windy City for a reason," Tony said.

"I'll bet you can't wait to get back to the West Coast," Rob said, and she shot him a sideways glance, as if to say, *Don't you wish.*

"I think I'll like it here," she said. "Though probably more when it warms up a little."

"Do you know where you'll be staying?" Nick asked.

"Not yet. I'm hoping to find a rental. I don't suppose you know a good local agent?"

"My brother-in-law David is in real estate law," Tony said, pulling out his phone. "He could probably give you the name of someone reliable."

He found the number in his address book, and she entered it into her phone.

"I miss the days when we used to write things on paper," Nick said.

"Have you got a piece of paper?" Rob asked, and grinning, Nick held up his napkin. "Pen?"

Nick felt his pockets, then frowned and said, "I used to carry one all the time."

"I would be lost without my phone," Carrie said. "My whole life is in this thing. Of course I keep it all backed up on my laptop, which I also could not live without."

"So what kind of place are you looking for?" Nick asked.

"A two-bedroom apartment or condo, preferably furnished, in a building with a fitness room and a pool, or close to a pool. I like to swim every morning."

"I think I may know just the place," Nick said. "My wife, Terri, has a condo that she's been thinking of putting on the market, but it would probably mean taking a loss. She had entertained the idea of renting it out, but she's heard so many horror stories about bad tenants that she's been hesitant. It has pretty much everything you would need, and there's a fitness center with a pool a couple of blocks away. And it's not too far from work."

It also wasn't too far from Rob's loft, which didn't exactly thrill him.

"It sounds perfect," Carrie said. "I can pay her the full three months up front."

"I'll talk to her today and give you a call."

"Sounds great," she said, exchanging numbers with him, which irritated Rob even more. It was bad enough that she would be around for three months. Did she have to pretend to be so nice to everyone? Which she was clearly only doing to make Rob look like the bad guy.

"So, on the rare occasions that I might have a free day," Carrie said, "what attractions would you gentlemen recommend? There are so many things to do in the city, I wouldn't even know where to begin."

His cousins tossed around suggestions like the planetarium and the aquarium and the Museum of Contemporary Art.

"How about you?" she asked Rob. "What would you suggest?"

"The Museum of Science and Industry."

"Really," she said, looking thoughtful. "For some reason I imagined your preferring someplace a little less... academic. Like a sports museum."

"And you assumed that because, why? You know me so well?"

She looked amused, as if this was some big joke to her.

The waitress dropped their food off at the table and when Rob looked at Carrie's plate, he could feel his arteries tighten. The special consisted of three eggs, four sausage links, hash browns, white toast and a stack of pancakes six inches high. A heart attack on a plate, his fitness instructor would call it. Which was why Rob had ordered his usual egg white vegetarian omelet, lean ham, tomato slices and dry whole wheat toast, of which he would allow himself half a slice. Unlike some people at the table, his goal was to live past his fortieth birthday.

"Do the three of you live in the city?" she asked them, and when her leg bumped his, he wrote it off as accidental, until he felt the brush of one shoeless foot slide against his ankle.

Was she coming onto him?

He shot her a sideways glance, but she was looking at Nick, chewing and nodding thoughtfully as she listened to him describe where each of them lived in relation to Caroselli Chocolate.

Okay, maybe it had been an accident. But what about

the way she just happened to get syrup on her fingers, and instead of wiping them with a napkin, sucked it slowly from each digit, one at a time. Which of course reminded him of her sucking on something else.

He grabbed his iced water and guzzled half the glass.

"Not hungry?" Carrie asked, looking over at his untouched food. He'd been so busy obsessing over her that he hadn't even thought about his breakfast.

"Letting it cool," he told her, forking up a large bite and shoveling it in, burning the hell out of his tongue in the process.

"So I'm under the impression you three aren't just cousins, but good friends," Carrie said.

"What makes you think that?" Tony asked.

"I'm very intuitive about things like that."

"Not so much when we were younger," Nick said. "Mostly because of the age difference, but our family is very close-knit, so we saw each other constantly. But, yeah, we're all pretty close now."

"So, then I guess Robby told you that we had sex on New Year's Eve."

Rob dropped his fork halfway to his mouth, Nick choked on his eggs and Tony nearly sprayed the table with a mouthful of coffee.

"What makes you think I would do that?" Rob said, even though that was exactly what he had done.

She smiled serenely. "As I said, I'm intuitive about that sort of thing."

"He may have mentioned it," Tony said, shrugging apologetically to Rob.

"I hope he also mentioned that we didn't know who the other was until this morning."

"That was fairly obvious," Nick said. "And you really don't have to explain."

"I prefer to get things out in the open. I wouldn't want anyone getting the wrong impression."

"Of course not," Tony said.

"Carrie," Rob started, and she held a hand up to shush him.

"I'm not angry," she said. "Men like to talk about their conquests, I get that. Hell, I called my friend Alice first thing the next morning. It's not as if we ever expected to see each other again. I'd just appreciate if it didn't go any further than this table."

"No one will hear it from me," Tony said.

"Me neither," Nick piped in, looking amused. "What you two do in your free time is no one else's business."

Was she doing this here, now, only so that she would have witnesses? So that if he promised not to say anything, then did, it would make him look like an even bigger jerk than he already might be.

She was good at this. But so was he.

"While we're being so honest, should we tell them what happened in my office this morning?"

Tony shot him a look. "Really not necessary."

"You mean what didn't happen," she said and told Nick and Tony with regret, "We ran out of time."

Both men looked to Rob, waiting for his reply, because obviously he hadn't gotten the response he'd hoped for by putting her on the spot. Did nothing rattle her?

"And it won't be happening again," he said, establishing that he was the one to end it, not her.

"And of course I understand why," she said. "I've learned from experience that it's a terrible idea to engage in a physical relationship with a coworker, especially a subordinate."

Subordinate? She was the subordinate, the temporary

consultant. Did she honestly see herself as ranking higher than him?

"I'd like your opinion on something," Carrie said, leaning forward to address Nick and Tony. "Say you have a one-night stand with a woman. You both know that it's never going to be more than one night. Now, it's the wee hours of the morning, she's asleep and you decide to go. Do you wake her and say goodbye, or maybe leave a note? Or do you just leave without a word?"

Nick glanced over at Rob. "I might get my ass kicked for saying this, but I would definitely wake her and say goodbye."

Carrie turned to Tony. "And you?"

"I would at least leave a note."

Carrie looked over at Rob and gave him a "so there" look.

"Boy, would you look at the time," Nick said, glancing at his wrist when, ironically enough, he wasn't wearing a watch. "Tony, we've got the thing we need to get to."

For an instant Tony looked confused, then he said, "Oh yeah, right, that *thing*. Of course. We wouldn't want to be late for that."

Nick grabbed the check that the waitress had left on the table.

"Here, let me give you cash for mine," Carrie said, reaching into her bag.

"Oh no, this one is on me," Nick said as he and Tony slid out of the booth.

"Thank you," she said. "I'll buy next time."

If there ever was a *next time,* they could count Rob out.

"You two enjoy the rest of your breakfast," Tony told them. As if Rob had any appetite left.

As soon as they were gone he switched to the empty side of the booth, which was actually worse than sitting beside Carrie. The deep cleft of cleavage at the low-cut collar of her top drew his gaze like a moth to a flame. The dull light leaking through the open blinds gave her pale gray eyes an almost-translucent quality.

"Well, that was fun," Carrie said.

"Amused yourself, did you?"

She smiled, sliding her empty plate to the edge of the table as the busboy cleared the dirty dishes and utensils. She sure could put away the food. She had stopped just shy of licking her plate clean.

"Tony and Nick seem like really nice guys," Carrie said. "I take it Tony isn't married."

"No, he isn't."

"Single?"

"Why? Are you interested?"

She cocked her head slightly. "Why? Are you jealous?"

"He just came out of a relationship, and the last thing he needs is someone like you messing with his head."

"Is that what I'm doing?" she asked, resting her elbow on the table and propping her chin in her hand. Then he felt a shoeless foot sliding up his left calf.

Damn her.

When she'd made it up to his knee, and clearly had no intention of stopping, he grabbed her stocking foot and removed it from his leg with a warning look, thankful for his long wool coat to hide anything that had *sprung up.* "You're taking cheap shots."

"Am I?"

"You don't really believe that I'm your subordinate."

The head cocked again. "When did I say that?"

"Just a minute ago. You said it was especially bad to get involved with a subordinate."

"So, from that you assumed I meant you? Had you considered that I was talking *to* you *about* me? Or that maybe

I was speaking in general terms, and not about anyone specific."

Actually no, he hadn't considered that.

"Are you always so hyperdefensive?" she asked.

"Never." Only when he was with her.

"Like I said, this will be as easy or as hard as you decide to make it." Her brow lifted slightly, but by the time he recognized the devilish look on her face, it was too late. He sucked in a surprised breath when he felt her still shoeless foot slide into his lap. "Hard, it is," she said with a smile.

"Would you stop that," he hissed, shoving her foot away from his crotch, hoping no one sitting nearby noticed. Did the woman have no shame? And why could he not think of anything but getting her back to her hotel room, out of her clothes and into bed? "Is this your idea of acting like a professional?"

"I'm simply trying to illustrate a point."

"What point? You're certifiable?"

"That when it comes to our relationship, work or otherwise, you do not always call the shots. Because, Robby, you have some *serious* control issues."

"*I* have control issues? This from the woman who can't keep her foot out of my crotch?"

She just smiled, as if she found the entire situation thoroughly amusing. "I'm going to go. I'll see you bright and early Monday."

"Unfortunately, yes, you will."

She pulled on her suit jacket and coat, and he watched her as she grabbed her bag, slid out of the booth and walked to the door. She stepped outside, her loose hair flying wildly in the brisk wind. She hailed a cab, and only after she climbed inside could he drag his gaze away from the window.

Unpredictable. That's what she was. And while he was

nowhere close to the control freak she'd painted him to be, he did prefer a modicum of consistency.

And if today's behavior was a preview of what he had to look forward to, maintaining control of the situation was his only option.

Five

Carrie sat at the hotel bar, having a celebratory margarita, which at 12:04 p.m. was completely acceptable, even though her internal clock still thought it was two hours earlier.

Even though there had been a few kinks in the process, all in all, she considered this morning's meeting a success. And though she had the tendency—in her stepfather's opinion—to be "mouthy," she felt that under the circumstances, she'd been impressively diplomatic. If she'd left out the part where they attacked each other in Rob's office.

The memory made her cringe. But she had regrouped, damn it, then gone back into that conference room and kicked some major Caroselli ass.

She'd found that in business, her impulsive nature could either be an asset or a liability, with very little gray area. This assignment could be a raging success, or a knock-down, drag-out disaster. So far so good, but honestly, it could still go either way. She had broken the cardinal rule of not sleeping with a coworker. And even though she had done it unknowingly, that didn't make the situation any less complicated.

As much as she hated to admit it, that stunt she'd pulled in the diner could have easily backfired. If he hadn't pulled her foot from his crotch, if he'd instead smiled and suggested they go back to her hotel room, she probably would have dragged him there by his tie. And though the cab ride there would have given them both time to come to their senses, the damage would have been done, and the ball would be in his court now.

Fortunately, the next serve was hers, and she was going for the point.

She licked salt off the rim of her glass and took a sip of her margarita, letting the tangy combination of sweet and salty roll around on her tongue. She glanced over at the businessman three barstools away, who she suspected had been working up the nerve to talk to her.

"Buy you a drink?" he said the instant they made eye contact.

Not only was he twice her age with thinning hair and a belly that sagged over his belt, but he also wore a chunky gold wedding band on his left hand.

Seriously? Did she really look that desperate?

She shook her head and gave him her not-in-this-lifetime look.

Her phone rang and, happy for the interruption, she dug around in her briefcase to find it, smiling when she saw her best friend Alice's number on the screen.

"So how did the meeting go?" Alice asked, and Carrie could picture her stretched out on the sofa in the trendy SoHo loft she shared with her sister, her glossy black hair smooth and sleek and tucked behind her ears. She never sat on a piece of furniture so much as draped herself across it.

At five feet eleven inches, and no more than one hundred and twenty pounds soaking wet, to say that Alice was wispy was an understatement. Hence her very lucrative career as a runway model. In college, where they'd been thrown together by chance as roommates, they had been like Mutt and Jeff. Two women could not have been more different in looks or personality, but with their similar backgrounds involving alcoholic parents, they had instantly bonded and despite living on completely opposite ends of the country, had remained the best of friends. Alice was her only *real* friend.

Normally Alice would be calling her from Milan or Paris or some other fashionably hip location, but a healing broken foot would be keeping her off the runway until the fall.

"They signed the contracts," Carrie told her. "So I'm in Chicago for the next three months."

"That's fabulous!"

"They didn't haggle over money either, which you know I hate. As far as business goes, the meeting itself couldn't have gone more smoothly."

"But?"

"What makes you think there's a but?"

"Gut feeling. I'm right, aren't I?"

She sighed. "I broke my cardinal rule. But it was an accident."

"I must be thinking of a different cardinal rule, because I fail to see how it's possible to *accidentally* sleep with someone."

"Nope, that's the rule. And I'm living proof that it is possible."

"Oh, I can't wait to hear this," Alice said, and Carrie

could just picture her catlike grin, the spark of amusement in her violet eyes—colored contacts of course, although she would deny it if asked.

"It's a little hard to believe," Carrie told her.

"Honey," she said with a laugh, "coming from you, I'd believe just about anything."

"That guy I told you about—Ron."

"Mr. Steamy Sex from the bar?"

"Yeah, well, apparently I heard him wrong. His name was actually *Rob*."

"Oh. And that's a problem because?"

"His name is Rob *Caroselli*. And he's the director of marketing at Caroselli Chocolate."

Alice was a tough person to shock, so her gasp was almost worth the mess Carrie was in.

Okay, maybe not, but it was at least a slight consolation.

Carrie told her the whole story, from the minute Rob walked into the conference room until lunch when she had her foot in his lap.

"Well, you were right about one thing," Alice said. "If anyone but you had told me that story, I doubt I would have believed them. But as impulsive as you are—"

"I'm not *that* impulsive," she argued, signaling the bartender for another drink.

"Your first night in a new city you picked up a total stranger in a bar and invited him back to your room."

Carrie cringed. "Yeah, there was that."

"Not that I'm saying you could have or should have anticipated this happening. That part was just dumb luck. Really, really bad dumb luck."

"But on the bright side, I think that now I've got him right where I want him."

"Until you wind up in bed with him again," Alice said.

"I can't sleep with him again."

"You mean you *shouldn't* sleep with him. Yet you almost went for it in his office this morning. Correct?"

"A moment of weakness. I was still getting over the shock of seeing him again."

"And in the diner?"

"I was making a point."

"And did you make your point?"

"I sure did." Below the waist anyway. "Why do I get the feeling I'm going to regret telling you any of this?"

"Because you know that if I think you're acting like an irresponsible moron, I'm going to tell you."

"And you think I am?"

"I think that you might be backsliding a little. Just remind yourself, you are no longer that lonely little girl who pulls fire alarms and stays out past curfew to get attention. You are a strong, mature woman who is in control of her own destiny."

"I know." But that little girl was still in there, and occasionally she persuaded the confident, mature woman to do some not-so-mature things. "The weird part is that I don't even like him very much. But then I get close to him and I just want to rip his clothes off and touch him all over."

"Probably not a good idea. You know, Rex and I used to have chemistry like that."

Alice's boyfriend, Rex, was an up-and-coming fashion designer whose rising star seemed to be keeping him out of the country more than he was in it lately. And even when he was in town, she didn't seem truly happy.

"When will he be back in New York?" Carrie asked.

"Two weeks. This time he promised."

He had promised her lots of things, and so far he hadn't exactly come through. Alice was beautiful and sophisticated and smart, but had miserably low self-esteem. Because of that, she let the men in her life walk all over her.

All types of men clamored for her attention, yet she always picked the aloof, distant ones whose attention she had to beg for. A fact she was quite aware of. But as Carrie had told Rob, a person could recognize the problem and still not know how to fix it.

"How's the foot healing?" Carrie asked her.

"Slowly. The physical therapy is helping. My doctor assured me that I'll be back on my feet before the shows next fall. It's crazy how you can be walking down the sidewalk, minding your own business, then *pow,* out of nowhere everything changes."

The *pow* in that scenario being the bike messenger who knocked her off the curb into the path of a moving taxi. She was lucky to be alive.

"And speaking of therapy," Alice said, "I have an appointment in an hour, so I should let you go. But I want you to make me a promise. If you get even the slightest urge to jump Mr. Steamy Sex again, I want you to call me immediately so I can talk some sense into you. Anytime, day or night."

"Okay."

"You promise?"

She sighed.

"Carrie?"

"Okay, okay, I promise," she said, hoping it wasn't one of those promises that came back to bite her in the butt.

Two days later Carrie hopped in a cab to meet Nick's wife, Terri, at the condo she hoped would be her new temporary home.

She was pleasantly surprised when the cab pulled up in front of a row of attached, newish-looking, charming brick homes with two-car garages. So far so good.

The homes were still decorated for the holidays. All but

the one the driver stopped at. Which wasn't so unusual considering no one was living there. Still, it looked so forlorn and neglected. But thankfully very well-maintained. At least on the outside.

She paid the driver, realizing that if she didn't want to blow her entire earnings on cab fare, it might be more cost effective to lease a car while she was there. She didn't exactly relish the thought of taking public transportation in the dead of winter either.

She climbed out of the cab and paused on the sidewalk to look up and down the street. All the residences were well-maintained, and a large group of children of various ages played in the snow several doors down, which led her to assume the neighborhood was family-oriented and safe.

She headed up the walk and as she stepped up onto the porch, the front door opened and a woman appeared to greet her.

"Hi. Caroline?"

"Carrie," she said, shaking her hand.

"I'm Terri. Come on in." Like her husband, Terri was tall and dark. She was also very attractive in an athletic, tomboyish way, and not at all the sort of woman she would have pictured Nick with. "Drop your coat anywhere and I'll give you a tour."

Carrie's first impression, as she stepped inside and shrugged out of her coat, was *beige*. Beige walls, beige carpet, beige leather furniture. Even the lamps were beige. And the air smelled like pine cleaner.

"As you can see, I left almost everything here when I moved into Nick's place," she said. "It's nothing fancy."

Carrie draped her coat over the back of the sofa beside Terri's and set her purse on top. "It's nice."

"According to Nick, to say I have the decorating sense of a brick is an insult to bricks."

"I'm no decorating genius either. I paid someone to do my place in Los Angeles. This is simple. Elegant."

"It's boring," Terri said. "And if you don't like it, don't be afraid to say so. You won't hurt my feelings."

She wasn't looking for anything fancy. Just something functional and low-maintenance that wouldn't break the bank. "So far so good."

Terri looked surprised. "You want to see more?"

"Absolutely." She could hate the rest of the condo and she would probably rent it anyway rather than hurt Terri's feelings.

Carrie had a way of reading people, and her first impression of Terri was that she had a tough outer shell but was soft and vulnerable on the inside.

The master suite had slightly more color. A queen-size bed with a pale rose duvet, a chest of drawers in a warm honey pine and a roomy walk-in closet that led to a very clean—and yes, beige—en suite bathroom that smelled of bleach and glass cleaner. The only color was pale pink towels and a pink bath mat. The countertops and walls were bare.

"There are towels, sheets…everything you'll need in the linen closet. I just changed the sheets on the bed and scrubbed the bathroom." Terri smiled sheepishly. "I'm slightly fanatical about keeping things clean and tidy."

"Linen closet?" Carrie asked, gesturing to a pair of louvered doors.

"Laundry." She pulled the doors open to show Carrie a stacked washer and dryer.

"Nice." She didn't miss the days before she had money, when she had to haul her dirty laundry down three flights of stairs and either sit in a dingy little laundry room down below the building in the parking structure, or drive two miles to the nearest Laundromat.

The second bedroom was set up as an office, with a desk, bookcase, file cabinet and printer stand. Again, nothing fancy, but very functional, and the window overlooked a postage-stamp-sized backyard.

"This is perfect," she told Terri.

"This room, you mean?"

"No, the whole place. It's exactly what I need."

"You really think so?"

"I do. Can I see the kitchen?"

"Of course. Right this way."

The kitchen, which was—surprise—also on the pale side, was as clean and organized as the rest of the house, and separated by a wall from the living space. She preferred a more open concept, but how much time would she be spending there really?

"I don't cook, so it's not very impressive," Terri said. "Just your basic pots and pans, dishes and utensils."

"I don't cook very often either," Carrie told her. "I like to, but I never have the time. I typically work eighty-hour weeks."

"I used to be like that, too, but my ob-gyn thinks all the stress is screwing with my cycle, and we're trying to get pregnant. So, I cut my hours way back. Used to be, when you opened the freezer it was full of frozen dinners. Thank goodness for husbands who love to cook. Although I've gained about ten pounds since the wedding."

"How long have you been married?"

"Less than two months."

"Oh, so you're still newlyweds."

"Technically. But we've been best friends since we were nine years old. And I don't want to be one of those moms in her fifties carting her kids to grade school, or pushing seventy when they graduate high school. For a process that's supposed to be so natural, you would not believe how complicated it can be."

It wasn't something Carrie had ever thought about. She didn't know much about pregnancy, or even babies. She just assumed that when you were ready, you had sex at the right time and *poof,* you got pregnant. That was the way it seemed to work for her college friends who had gotten married and started families. Hell, there were even a handful of girls in high school who seemed to have no problems getting themselves knocked up. A few of them multiple times.

"So what do you think of the condo?" Terri asked. "Again, I won't be insulted if you don't like it, or if you'd like to look at other places before making a decision."

"I think," Carrie said with a smile, "I'll take it."

Six

"You're sure?" Terri asked.

Carrie laughed. "Yes, I'm very sure. Did you bring a lease agreement?"

"It's in my coat. I'll get it."

They took a seat at the kitchen table and went over the paperwork. When it came to filling in the price of rent, Terri looked over at her. "So we're talking rent plus utilities, including cable TV and internet."

"Name your price," Carrie told her, and she offered up a sum that seemed awfully low for all of that, especially in the heart of a major city. "Are you sure you don't want more? I don't expect any sort of special treatment. I want to pay what's fair."

"Nick and I talked about it. We're not looking to make a profit, just cover expenses."

"You're positive?"

She nodded. "That's the way things are done in the

Caroselli family. They're a very generous bunch. They suck people into the fold."

"Is a personal check okay?"

"If it bounces, I'll know where to find you," Terri joked.

Carrie wrote the check out for three months' worth of rent, tore it from the book and handed it to Terri, feeling guilty to be paying such a low sum.

"Are you sure you want to pay all three months up front?"

"It's just easier for me that way. One less thing I have to worry about remembering." She slid her checkbook back into her bag. "So when you said that the Carosellis *suck* people in, what exactly did you mean by that?"

She must have looked apprehensive because Terri chuckled and said, "Don't worry, it's nothing creepy or weird. Take me, for example. When I moved to Chicago, I was nine. I had just lost my parents and I was living with an aunt who wasn't exactly thrilled to play Mommy to some bratty kid she had never met before. I guess you could say that I was a lost soul. Then I became friends with Nick, and I met his family, and it was like they adopted me. Nick likes to joke that if his mom had to choose between the two of us, she would pick me."

"That's really nice," Carrie said. "Everyone should have family."

"Do you have a big family?"

"I have a few cousins, and a couple of aunts and uncles spread out across the southwest, but I haven't seen them in years. Mostly it's just me and my mom."

"You're close?" she asked, and when Carrie didn't answer right away, Terri said, "I'm sorry, it's really none of my business. The Carosellis are also very nosy, and I guess it rubbed off on me."

"It's okay. It's just that my relationship with my mom

is a little…complicated. We don't really see each other very often. I work a lot and she spends most of her time in a bottle."

Terri nodded. "Ah, I see."

"There's a lot of resentment from my end, and apathy from hers. I have the typical characteristics of a child with an alcoholic parent." She paused and said, "Was that too much information?"

"No, not at all. I didn't even know there were typical characteristics. Which ones do you have, if you don't mind my asking?"

"I'm super-responsible and I take myself way too seriously. Your basic overachiever. When I'm trying to have fun, I feel as if I should be doing something more constructive. But due to a lack of self-esteem, I feel that nothing I do is good enough. I also have trust issues, so I have trouble forming intimate relationships. And telling you all of this is probably just some unconscious way of mine to push you away before I'm able to form any sort of friendship or bond."

"Wow, that's intense," Terri said.

"Yeah, those psych courses I took in college were a real eye-opener. Up until then, under the circumstances, I figured I was fairly well-adjusted. Psychology was actually my major for a while, until it dawned on me that no one as screwed up as I was had any right to be counseling anyone else. That's an enormous responsibility and there was no way I could trust myself to be completely impartial. So I switched my major to marketing. I'm still using what I learned about psychology, without the possibility of screwing with someone's head." She paused and said, "Well, not in a bad way at least. I just encourage them to buy stuff."

"It seems as though you aren't so screwed up that you

didn't realize you're screwed up." Terri frowned. "Does that make sense?"

"It does, actually."

"Hey, do you have plans for tomorrow night?"

Her first thought was of Rob, which was wrong in so many ways. "Nope. I don't really know anyone in the city."

"Nick and I are having some friends over and I'd really like you to come."

"Really? After everything I just told you?"

"Oh, don't worry. You'll fit right in."

Carrie wasn't quite sure how to take that, then decided it was probably meant as a compliment. "In that case, I'd love to."

"It's at seven," she said, writing down the address. "Do you have a way to get there?"

"I can take a cab."

"Or I could ask Rob to swing by and pick you up. It's on his way."

"Oh, I think it would be better if I took a cab."

"If you're worried about getting home safe, Rob isn't much of a drinker. Come to think of it, I don't recall ever seeing him drunk."

"The night I met him he drank a lot," Carrie said, not even realizing what she was saying until the words left her mouth. Everyone was supposed to think their first meeting was in the conference room.

"Yeah, I heard," Terri said.

She blinked. "You did?"

"Word of advice, if you don't want me to know something, don't tell Nick. We're one of those couples who actually tell each other everything."

"Good to know." Carrie recalled the way she had announced to the entire table at the diner about her and Rob's affair, *and* what happened in Rob's office, meaning Terri probably knew about that, too.

Way to go, genius. What had Alice said about her impulsive tendencies? She really needed to think things through before she opened her mouth. She wondered how many others in the Caroselli family knew.

"Did he happen to tell anyone else?" she asked Terri.

"I doubt it. And I don't think Tony would tell anyone either."

She hoped not. She didn't want people to get the impression she slept around, because nothing could be further from the truth.

"For the record, that's not typical behavior for me," she told Terri.

"And for what's it worth, it's not typical behavior for him either," Terri said. "You must have made quite an impression on him. Personally, I think you two make an adorable couple."

"Oh, but we aren't. A couple, I mean. I make it a rule not to date people I work with. If I'd had even the slightest clue as to who he was when I met him in that bar—"

"Carrie, I understand. Believe me. Maybe it was just… fate."

If it was, fate had played a very cruel trick on both of them. "We couldn't be more wrong for each other. In more ways than I can even count."

"Six months ago, if you had told me I would be married to Nick and trying to have a baby, I would have thought you were nuts. Yet here we are."

"So what happened? What changed?"

"That is a very long story, and I promise to tell you about it when you come to the party tomorrow."

"I hardly know you and you're already blackmailing me?"

Terri smiled wryly. "It's the Caroselli way."

"I'll definitely be there, but I'll find my own ride."

"Well, I should go," Terri said. "If there's anything you need, or if you have a question, just give me or Nick a call."

"It was really nice talking to you," Carrie told her.

"I think so, too," Terri said, looking a little embarrassed. She struck Carrie as the type who probably had more male than female friends. While Carrie had very few of either.

"And thanks for the advice," Carrie said.

"Anytime." Terri pulled on her coat, then fished a set of keys from her pocket and handed them to Carrie. "Those open the front and garage door."

"Thanks. See you tomorrow."

When she was gone, Carrie started to explore the kitchen cabinets, feeling a little like a snoop. But she was sure that Terri would have removed anything of a personal nature before she rented out the condo.

She opened the refrigerator and smiled. On the shelf sat an unopened half gallon of low-fat milk, a dozen organic eggs and a loaf of organic nine-grain bread. One shelf down was a bottle of very expensive champagne.

Terri had gone above and beyond to make her feel welcome, and Carrie hoped they would have time to get to know one another better.

Carrie returned to the hotel to collect her things, then took a cab back to the condo, doing her best to memorize the street names so she could find her way around when she had a car. It had begun to snow, so rather than have the driver track it through the living room and potentially ruin the carpet, she had him leave the bags in the garage.

She opened the door to total darkness, cursing herself for not remembering to leave a light on. She felt around on the inside wall for a light switch. She found it and as she was flipping it upward, she felt a cold hand settle on top of hers.

She shrieked and yanked her hand back, the bright light temporarily blinding her. She blinked hard and when she opened her eyes again, no one was there. She peeked around the corner, but the only thing there was a door. Probably to the basement.

She took a slow, deep breath to calm her pounding heart. It was just her imagination. No one was there. She'd clearly been watching too many episodes of *Ghost Hunter*.

She turned to grab her bags, nearly colliding with the very large person standing there. She shrieked again, then realized that it was only Rob.

"You scared me half to death!" she said.

He wore a long black wool coat and black leather gloves…and an amused grin. Fat flakes of snow dotted his dark hair and he'd left snowy footprints on the garage floor. "A little jumpy?"

"What do you want?"

"What made you scream?"

"*You* did!"

"No, the first time."

"Nothing. I was imagining things."

"Imagining what?"

She shook her head. "*Nothing*. It wasn't real."

He narrowed his eyes. "What wasn't real?"

She blew out an exasperated breath. "If you must know, when I reached around for the light switch, I could swear somebody put their hand over mine, but when I turned on the light, no one was there."

"It must have been the lady in the basement."

She blinked. "The *who?*"

"We call her the lady in the basement. Not everyone senses her. Terri and Nick never did, but a lot of other people have. Sometimes she touches people, some people hear her walking up and down the stairs. Some hear her crying. I smell her perfume."

She couldn't tell if he was being serious or just messing with her. "Really?"

"I can smell it from the instant I step in the garage door until I step into the kitchen. Maybe three feet. Then it's gone. I've felt her brush against me, and once I felt a hand on my shoulder."

"No way." She leaned into the doorway and sniffed, but all she smelled was pine cleaner and bleach.

"You have to actually step inside," Rob said. "Or it doesn't work."

She eyed him skeptically. Had she honestly just rented a house with a dead lady living in the basement? And wasn't that sort of thing supposed to be disclosed before the lease was signed? Or was Rob just full of it?

Of course he was.

"You're lying," she said.

"I'm dead serious. Try it if you don't believe me."

It was walk in this door or walk around to the front door, which would make her look even more ridiculous than she probably did now. So basically she was damned if she did and damned if she didn't.

Promising herself that no matter what happened she would not react, she lifted her foot and stepped up over the threshold, then followed with the opposite foot, and the second it touched the floor—

A hand clamped down over her shoulder, and even though deep down she knew it was Rob, a startled screech ripped from her throat.

Heart pounding, she spun around and gave him a hard shove. "You're an *ass*."

"And you are *way* too gullible," he said, laughing and shaking his head. "I can't believe you fell for that."

"I didn't think it was possible, but I like you even less than I did before."

"It was worth it to see the look on your face."

She stomped into the house and switched on the kitchen light, expecting him to follow. And he did, hauling two of her bags inside with him.

"What are you doing?"

"Where do you want them?" he asked.

She was about to tell him she would do it herself, then thought, what the heck. He might as well get used to following directions from her. "They all go in the bedroom."

He had clearly been there before, because he seemed to know where all the light switches and the bedrooms were located.

She shrugged out of her coat, wondering if she might find a box of tea bags somewhere.

On his second trip through to the bedroom, Rob asked, "Are you sure you packed enough stuff? These things weigh a ton."

"You try packing three months' worth of stuff," she called after him as he disappeared down the hall. "That's a long time to be away from home."

Two of the smaller bags had nothing in them but shoes. One was filled with casual clothes, though she realized now that much of it was too light for the cold weather. She would have to do some clothes shopping, and soon. The rest was work clothes, some of which were also inappropriate for the season. Living in a warmer climate, it was difficult to imagine how cold Midwestern winters could be.

"What are you doing here anyway?" she asked on his final trip back to the garage. "And how did you even know where I was?"

He walked back in with the last two bags. "I talked to Nick."

Of course he would know, because Terri told Nick everything. Not that it was some big secret. She just didn't want Rob thinking it was okay to come by and hassle her whenever he felt like it.

This time she followed him into the bedroom. He set her bags down with the others by the closet, then turned to her.

"Which doesn't explain why you're here," she said, folding her arms, giving him her stern look.

"To give you this." He tugged his gloves off, pulled a flash drive out of his inside coat pocket and handed it to her.

"What is it?"

"The financial reports you asked Elana for."

"Oh. She could have given them to me Monday."

He shrugged. "I figured you would probably want to get an early start on this."

Actually, no, she planned to start Monday, when her contract started. But it was interesting that Rob chose to bring it when he didn't have to.

"Thanks," she said, and crossed the room to set it on the nightstand. But when she turned back around, Rob was no longer standing by the closet. He was in front of the bedroom door, blocking her only exit from the room. And he was wearing that *look*.

All the parts of her that had been craving his touch shivered to attention. What on earth had possessed her to follow him in here? If there was a single worst place for them to be together, it was a bedroom.

Rolling her eyes in response to the visual overture, she walked over to her bags and grabbed one that was filled with shoes. She went into the closet with it, found a good place to put them, then bent at the waist to unzip the bag—

and not just because she was trying to make her butt look good either. One by one she pulled the shoes out, pairing them together on the floor.

She heard him in the bedroom, just outside the closet, the hiss of his arms through the satin lining of his coat sleeves. Okay, so he was taking his coat off. That didn't mean he would try anything. He had been the one to proclaim that it was over the other morning. What was he going to do? Break his own rules? Although it would be fun to turn the tables again and turn him down.

She could do that. Right? All she had to do was call Alice and she would talk her out of it.

Before she could make up her mind, she felt his hands slide around her hips, his fingers gripping as he rubbed his crotch across her behind. He was already noticeably turned on, and she wasn't faring much better.

"Really," she said, looking back at him. "This is so… cliché."

"You're one to talk." He slid his fingers under the hem of her sweater, brushing them across her bare skin. "Besides, you didn't seem to mind it like this the other night."

No, she hadn't, had she? And it was very cliché of him to remind her.

Where the hell was her phone? She needed to call Alice pronto.

As she straightened up, he slid his hands around to her belly, pulling her back against him. Oh, that was nice. But not half as nice as when his hands slid up to cup her breasts a second after.

She sighed and let her head drop back against his chest. "I distinctly recall your telling me that this was not going to happen again. And you were right."

"Well, I changed my mind."

"You can't do that."

"I just did." He tucked her hair to one side, kissed the back of her neck, the heat from his body melting her brain.

"We're coworkers," she reminded him.

"Technically we're not. Not yet. Your contract doesn't officially begin until Monday."

He made a valid point. And because they had already slept together, the pre-working-relationship part was already a lost cause. Right?

So what was the big deal if they did it one more time? If she held it up beside the "big picture," it was a tiny, tiny thing. Barely a blip. And why bother Alice when this was clearly going to be the last time?

His hands were under her sweater now, his hot palms scorching a path across her skin. He nibbled the side of her neck, then sucked hard.

A guy hadn't given her a hickey since she was fifteen, but it was unbelievably erotic to think that he was marking her, branding her as his.

She turned to face him, sliding her arms around his neck. "Okay, but just this one time, and that's it."

"Agreed. Unless we have to do it again tomorrow, because it's only Saturday. Then of course there's Sunday…"

"But not after Monday."

"Definitely." He lifted her right off her feet and carried her to the bed. There was no better way to make a house feel like a home than to have really awesome sex in it.

Seven

Rob tossed her not so gently onto the mattress and pulled his shirt up over his head.

She pulled her shirt off, too, then her bra. "For the record, I still don't like you."

"I know," he said, red-hot lust in his eyes as he unfastened his pants. "Take off your jeans."

She unfastened them and shoved them down, and his dropped to the floor. His pants *and* his underwear.

"This is just sex," she told him, as he tugged her panties down her legs. "We're not friends."

"Definitely not." He knelt at the end of the mattress and began to kiss his way up her legs, pushing them apart as he worked his way higher, and when he reached the apex of her thighs, he kissed her there, then took her into his mouth.

She had forgotten that he had such a talented tongue. But as good as it was, she wanted him inside her when she came, and he must have been thinking the same thing. He moved over her, settled between her open thighs, his weight pressing her into the mattress in the most appealing way.

He took her hands in his and pinned them over her head. "Tell me you want me."

"This was your idea," she said. "So clearly you're the one who wants *me*."

He lowered his head to lick her nipple, then suck it into his mouth. *Hard.* She gasped and pushed up against his grip.

"Tell me you want me," he said, and the devilish look in his eyes said he would take whatever measures necessary to make her cooperate…like slide his erection against her, teasing her with the tip, until she was restless and needy.

"Fine, I want you," she said, shifting underneath him.

His deadpan expression said that wasn't exactly what he'd had in mind. But there was something else, an undercurrent of emotion that made her wonder if he actually *needed* to hear it.

She looked into his eyes and said, "I want you."

With a swift and not-so-gentle thrust that stole her breath, he was inside of her. Then he pulled back and thrust again and pleasure rippled through her like a shock wave. A few more of those and it would be all over for her. She held her breath, anticipating the next thrust, but instead Rob stopped, cursing under his breath.

"Something wrong?" she asked him.

He looked down at her. "Are you using any kind of birth control?"

She shook her head.

"At present, neither am I, so before it's too late…"

She shoved him off her. "Yes, definitely. Please."

Thank goodness he'd noticed in time. She couldn't even imagine what a disaster it would have been if he hadn't. She was at the worst possible time in her cycle to be taking chances.

If there was a world speed record for rolling on a condom, she was sure he broke it. But this time, as he lowered himself over her, he took things a bit slower. Fast, slow, she didn't care, so long as he was touching her.

"You're so beautiful," he said, his eyes searching her face, as if he were trying to memorize her down to the tiniest detail. Hot friction burned at her core, mounting with every slow, steady thrust. She could feel the pleasure coiling tight, the pressure building. She was going to tell him that they needed to slow down, but it was already too late. Her body, her entire being was sucked under into a whirlpool of pleasure. Rob growled and tensed as he came.

And as good as it felt, she was almost sorry that it was over, that it hadn't lasted longer. Of course, if this was anything like that night in the hotel, they weren't anywhere near finished.

Carrie woke the next morning and sat up in bed, disoriented by the unfamiliar room. Then she remembered that she was living in the condo now. In Chicago.

And last night…

She looked over at the empty spot beside her and sighed. The son of a bitch had sneaked out on her again. She looked around for a note, but once again, he hadn't bothered to leave one.

It figured.

In a huff, she tugged on her robe and trudged sleepily to the kitchen to make a pot of coffee. There was a handwritten note stuck to the refrigerator door with a magnet:

Sorry, had to work. I had a great time last night.
Left at 7, no skulking involved. Wanna not be friends
again tonight after the party?

It was silly, but the fact that he'd listened, and really *heard* her, that he remembered to leave a note this time, and especially one so sweet and funny, made her dislike him a little less. And that scared her. What they were doing now was simple and impartial. It didn't mean anything, which made it very, very safe. But what if they really started to like each other?

Oh, what was she worried about? The next time she saw him he would say something rude or chauvinistic and she would be back to hating him.

Carrie showered and dressed, and was standing in the kitchen getting ready to call a cab to take her to the nearest mall when she heard a creaking sound, as if someone had opened the inside garage door. Expecting to see Rob, or even Terri, she stepped around the corner, but there was no one there and the door was still shut and locked from last night.

What the—

That was when she looked over at the basement door and realized it was open. But it had been closed and latched when they came in last night. She recalled feeling the hand over hers and her heart skipped a beat. It was possible that Rob had opened it this morning before he left. But why?

The more likely and logical explanation was that the door wasn't latched all the way and had drifted open.

She grabbed the doorknob and pulled it closed, making sure that it really latched this time. Feeling better, she called the cab and left to go shopping. She found herself some nice casual things, and most of them from the clearance rack.

She forgot all about the basement door until she was in the kitchen fixing herself a cup of hot tea later that evening, and she had the sudden, eerie sensation that someone was watching her.

She knew she was just imagining things, but feeling the tiniest bit apprehensive anyway, she edged her way over and peered around the edge of the wall…sighing with relief when she found the door firmly latched.

Of course it was still closed, and the hand she'd felt had just been her imagination. She felt silly for believing it could be anything else.

The kettle whistled, and she shut off the burner. She poured water into her cup, and was about to take a sip when she heard it. The distinct creak of a door.

No way. She had to be imagining it.

She forced herself to walk over and peek around the wall.

"I'll be damned," she said into the silence. The basement door was open again.

Rob knocked on Carrie's front door at ten minutes to seven.

She opened the door a crack and peeked out, blinking with surprise. "What are you doing here?"

"Picking you up for the party."

She narrowed her eyes at him. "I'm confused."

"The party at Nick and Terri's. You are going, aren't you?"

"Yes, but I told Terri I would find my own ride."

"Well, I didn't talk to Terri."

"Oh. So why are you here?"

"To save you cab fare. Because it was on my way. To be nice." He shrugged and said, "Pick one."

"To get laid."

"That would work, too." He stamped his feet to keep the blood from freezing in his veins. "Whatever it takes for you to let me inside before my feet freeze to the porch."

She hesitated. "We are not friends."

"I'm well aware of that."

She finally moved back to let him in. He stepped inside and she shut the door. When he saw what she was wearing, he nearly swallowed his own tongue. In a figure-hugging denim miniskirt, knee-high spike-heeled boots and a clingy pink sweater, she clearly had no qualms about showing off her figure. "Wow. You look nice."

"You don't think it's too much?"

Even if it was, he would pay her to keep wearing it. Each time he thought he'd seen her at her sexiest, she managed to outdo herself.

"If we drive there together, people are going to get the idea that we're a couple," she said.

He shrugged. "Does it really matter what anyone thinks?"

"It's different for you. You're a man. If you score with a woman at work, you're a stud. If I do that, I'm a slut."

"Really. Was there a particular woman at work that you're interested in?"

She rolled her eyes. "You know what I mean."

"We could just tell people the truth, and say that I picked you up because it was on my way. Or, if it makes you feel better, you can go in first, and I can come in a few minutes later."

"That could work," she said. "And even if people suspect we're together, they'll eventually get the idea that we don't like each other. At all."

"Exactly. Get your coat."

She hesitated. "Before we go, I have to ask you something."

"Okay."

"You have to promise not to make fun of me."

Oh, this should be good. "All right. I promise."

"When you told me that thing about the lady in the basement, you really were kidding, right?"

"Of course I was kidding. Why? Did you feel the hand again?"

"No, I did not."

"But something happened, didn't it?"

"At first I thought it was a fluke…"

"What?"

"The basement door has been sort of…opening by itself."

He cast her a disbelieving look.

"I'm dead serious. I close it, then check it a little while later, and it's open like an inch or two."

"You probably aren't latching it all the way."

"No, I most definitely did latch it."

"If you did, it wouldn't have opened."

She propped her hands on her hips, glaring at him. "Are you honestly suggesting that I am incapable of latching a door?"

It was more plausible than the door opening by itself. "Let's take a look at it," he said. She followed him through the kitchen, her heels clicking on the tile floor. The basement door was open about an inch.

"See?" she said. "I closed and latched it less than fifteen minutes ago."

She was letting her imagination get the best of her. He pulled it closed and made sure that it was latched securely. He tried to open it without turning the knob and it wouldn't budge. There was no way that door would open without someone physically turning the handle. "Okay," he said, watching the knob. "Let's see it open."

"It doesn't work that way. I sat and watched it for like fifteen minutes and it didn't move, so I walked away. Five minutes later it was open again."

"Then let's go in the other room."

"I have to finish getting ready."

He looked her up and down. "You look ready to me."

That earned him another eye roll. "If you want to drive me, you'll have to wait."

It wasn't that he wanted to drive her. It just seemed rude not to. And if it increased his chances of getting her naked again tonight, why the hell not?

Knowing how long women could take getting ready, he shrugged out of his coat and made himself comfortable on the sofa. After a moment or two, curiosity got the best of him. He pushed himself up from the sofa and quietly sneaked through the kitchen to look around the corner. The basement door was as he'd left it. He tried the knob and it was securely latched.

As he suspected, there were no supernatural forces at work here. She had probably been in a rush and hadn't latched it, or maybe she really didn't know how to properly latch a door.

He went and sat back down on the sofa to wait for her, checking the door two more times with the same results. It was still closed tight.

Carrie reemerged several minutes later, pulling on her coat. If she'd done anything different to her appearance, he couldn't tell. Maybe she was one of those women who just didn't feel the night was complete unless she made a man wait for fifteen or twenty minutes.

"So, did you check the door?" she asked him.

"Three times. It didn't budge."

Looking discouraged, she said, "I *swear* it opened by itself."

He shrugged. "I don't know what to say. If it had mysteriously opened I would have told you."

"I *did* close it all the way."

"Okay."

"But you don't believe me."

"I didn't say that."

"You didn't have to." Exasperated, she looked over at the clock and said, "We had better go."

She grabbed her clutch from the coffee table. "I want to go out the garage door so I can grab the opener. If we're going to 'not be friends' after the party tonight, I want you to put your car in the garage."

"Why?"

She shot him a look.

Clearly she didn't want anyone to know he was there. Like he would argue over such an inconsequential detail when sex was involved. "Fine. Paint it camouflage for all I care."

He grabbed his coat and was tugging it on as they walked through the kitchen to the garage door, and she stopped so abruptly that he actually ran into her.

"Rob, that's really not funny," she said, looking at the basement door. Someone or something must have been making a point because the door wasn't open an inch or two this time. It was open all the way.

Eight

"It opens by itself?" Terri looked as skeptical as Rob had when Carrie told him about the basement door. They stood in Terri and Nick's kitchen with several of their friends, including Tony's sister Elana, and a guy named Mark who was making no secret of the fact that he found Carrie attractive. He was cute in an average way. Average height, average weight, naturally blond hair that was thinning a bit on top. And though he went a little gung ho with the aftershave, he seemed very nice, if not slightly forward in his intentions. But when he stood close to her, the air didn't crackle with energy, and her heart didn't beat faster, and when he touched her arm, her skin didn't shiver with awareness. In other words, he was no Rob.

She had already formed a gentle rejection in case Mark asked her out. Which seemed inevitable at this point.

"I take it that never happened when you lived there," Carrie said.

Terri shrugged. "If it did I never noticed. Far as I remember, the door was always closed. I hardly ever go down there. I mostly just use it for storage."

"Storage of what?" Elana asked. "Human remains?"

Terri shot her a withering look. "Old furniture."

Lisa, who worked in Nick's department at Caroselli Chocolate, asked, "Haunted furniture?"

"Not that I know of. But some of it is pretty old. Things my aunt had in her attic when she died. Stuff that has been in the family for a couple hundred years. I doubt I'll ever use any of it, but it seemed wrong to sell it."

Carrie glanced over to the living room where Tony, Rob and a very attractive Asian woman Carrie hadn't yet been introduced to stood by the sofa talking. The woman had come to the party late, and whoever she was, Rob seemed utterly enthralled by what she was saying, hanging on her every word.

Abruptly, as if he'd sensed her eyes on him, Rob looked over at Carrie and caught her staring. The corner of his mouth tilted into a wry smile.

Even though they had arrived together, they hadn't said more than ten words to each other in the two hours they had been there. A few times when he'd walked past, his arm had brushed hers, and once, when they reached into the chips bowl at the same time, their fingers touched. He'd given her his "look" and all she'd been able to think about since then was how they would go back to her place and "not be friends" all night long.

As far as she had seen, Rob had been nursing the same drink since they arrived, confirming what Terri had told her about his not being much of a drinker. Carrie on the other hand was on her fourth glass of wine. Each time she drained her glass, Mark would automatically refill it.

She was beginning to think that he was trying to get her drunk. He seemed a bit tipsy himself.

"Anything else weird happen?" Terri asked her.

"There was one other thing. I was in the garage and reached inside to feel around for the light switch, and I felt a hand settle on top of mine. A very cold hand."

"Eew," Elana said with a shudder, rubbing her arms. "That just gave me goose bumps."

"Me, too," Terri said. "I definitely never experienced anything like that, and if I had, I think I probably would have moved. In fact, if you want to look for a different place, I totally understand."

"The idea that someone or something is there is a little creepy," Carrie admitted. "But I don't get a negative vibe. I don't feel threatened at all. Or even scared."

"Have you been down in the basement?" Mark asked.

"I don't know if I'm that brave," she said.

He slipped an arm around her shoulder, grinned down at her and said, "I'll protect you."

The strong scent of liquor on his breath actually burned her eyes. She waited for him to remove his arm, but he left it there. It didn't feel *awful* exactly. Just a little…awkward. And not sexually stimulating in the least. Which had her automatically looking over at Rob, who was leaning in somewhat close to the Asian woman. He laughed at something she said, then slipped an arm around her shoulder.

Carrie tried to ignore an annoying little jab of jealousy. Whom he did or didn't hook up with at a party was none of her business. Although at the rate things were going, she might be taking a cab home and spending the night alone. Which was fine. He hadn't promised that they would spend the night together. In fact, it was probably better if they didn't.

And if that was true, why did she feel so crummy?

"We should call a medium," Elana said.

"As opposed to a small or a large," Mark joked, but no one laughed.

Elana rolled her eyes. "Like the one on that cable show who talks to the dead."

"I've seen that show," Terri said. "But isn't she in New York?"

"Long Island," Elana said. "I wonder if there's a reputable one in Chicago?"

"Or maybe you need an exorcist," Mark joked, the weight of his arm making her shoulder ache. It seemed that now he was leaning on her more for support, to stay upright.

"Whatever it is, I don't think it's evil," Carrie said, shifting away, only to have him lean more heavily on her. She glanced over at Rob. He laughed at something the Asian woman said, then kissed her cheek.

Yep, she was definitely on her own tonight. She tried not to let herself feel too disappointed. It would have ended Sunday anyway.

"We should have a séance," Elana suggested. "Do they still sell Ouija boards? I used to have one when I was a kid. Until *Nonna* found it and freaked out. She was very superstitious."

"Did you ever actually talk to the spirits with it?" Lisa asked.

"We used to pretend we did to scare each other, but I'm pretty sure everyone was moving the little plastic thing on their own."

"Whatever it is down there, maybe disturbing it would be a bad idea," Terri said.

And because she was the one who lived there, Carrie added, "I agree. I have no problem sharing, as long as it stays in the basement. I'll stay out of its way if it stays out of mine."

She had that feeling of being watched, but when she turned to look at Rob, his attention was on his companion. All this talk of ghosts and the supernatural was making her paranoid.

The weight of Mark leaning on her shoulder was not only uncomfortable, but it was also starting to grate on her nerves, and his cloying aftershave was giving her a headache. At the risk of him falling over, she swiftly ducked from under his arm. He teetered, then caught his balance on the edge of the counter.

"Bathroom?" she asked Terri. She didn't have to go, but she needed a minute or two of fresh air.

"Down the hall on the left," Terri told her, "and if that one is busy, there's one in my office and another in the master bedroom, through the closet." She lowered her voice and said, "If Mark is annoying you, just tell him to back off. He's a decent guy when he's not drinking. Unfortunately, that isn't very often."

In that case, Carrie was less worried about hurting his feelings. The last thing she needed or wanted was another alcoholic in her life, complicating things. "Thanks, I will."

As she headed down the hall, her phone started to ring. She checked the display and saw that it was Alice. Again. Out of guilt she had been avoiding her calls. She would talk to her next week, when she could honestly say that she wasn't sleeping with Rob. It was just too difficult to explain.

The first bathroom was occupied, so she tried the door on the right at the end of the hall and found herself in the master bedroom. Feeling a little weird being in someone else's bedroom, she crossed the room and walked through the closet to the bathroom. She stepped inside and was about to close the door, when someone on the other side pushed it open. She felt a sudden stab of alarm, thinking it was probably Mark. But it was Rob who stepped inside.

"You startled me," Carrie said, a hand pressed over her cleavage, in the exact spot he wanted to bury his face.

"Were you expecting Mark?" Rob asked, closing and locking the door behind him. "You two were looking awfully cozy."

She folded her arms and stuck out her chin. "Jealous?"

"Not at all, because we both know he's not half the man that I am."

"Maybe I think he is," she said, but her eyes betrayed her, just as they had in the kitchen, when Mark was hanging all over her. He could tell that she was as annoyed as he had been.

"No, you don't. That's why you couldn't keep your eyes off me."

"What are you doing in here anyway? Shouldn't you be out talking to your girlfriend?"

He paused for a second, then said, "Don't worry, she'll be along in a minute. All three of us disappearing at the same time would be way too obvious."

All *three* of them? She blinked, then glanced at the door. "That had better be a joke."

"What's the matter?" he said, walking toward her, grinning when she backed away from him. "You don't like to share?"

"You're not funny, you know."

"My 'girlfriend' is Megan."

"Okay."

"Megan Caroselli. My sister."

She blinked again, looking confused, then said, "Oh."

"My *adopted* sister."

She nodded and said, "Okay," as if it suddenly made sense.

He stepped closer, backing her against the countertop. "I like that you were jealous, though."

"I was not jealous," she said, jutting that chin out again.

He wasn't buying the tough act. "You want me," he said.

She rolled her eyes. "Could you be more arrogant?"

He grinned, reaching up to cup her cheek in his palm, swiping his thumb across her lower lip. All he'd been able to think about since he showed up at her place was getting her out of her clothes and back into bed. Staying away from her all evening, pretending he wasn't lusting after her, had been torture. And apparently he hadn't done a very good job of hiding his feelings where Nick was concerned.

Nick had cornered him about an hour ago and said, "Why don't you go over and talk to her?"

"Who?" Rob asked.

"You know damn well who. You two can't keep your eyes off each other."

He didn't see any point in lying to his cousin. "She doesn't want people to think we're involved."

"Anyone with eyes and half a brain is going to eventually notice that you two are lusting after each other. Hell, the temperature in the room rises a good ten degrees when you get within five feet of each other."

Rob honestly hadn't realized it was so obvious, and had been diligent about not going near her or even looking at her for the past hour or so—which had been a lot more difficult than he would have anticipated. Especially when Mark started to put the moves on her. But it seemed as though the more Rob ignored her, the more he lusted for her. When she finally brushed Mark off, Rob had been about ten seconds from punching him in the nose. And though he hadn't actually planned to follow Carrie to the bathroom, his feet had carried him there.

"We can't do this here," Carrie said, yet when he leaned in and kissed the side of her neck, she put up zero resistance. "Someone will hear us."

"We'll be quiet," he said, nuzzling her ear, breathing in the scent of her perfume. "You smell good."

"Rob, stop."

He should have cared who heard, but he didn't. He turned her so she was facing the mirror, watched her over her shoulder. "Say that like you mean it and I will."

"I mean it," she said, but he could tell that she didn't. She just didn't want to admit it. Didn't want to let down her guard and surrender herself to the desire that was eating them both alive.

He reached around to cup her breasts, squeezing the firm mounds. She moaned and her eyes rolled closed. Her hands fisted stubbornly rather than touch him, but they didn't push him away either. He couldn't be in the same room with her for very long without putting his own hands all over her. Which could be a major problem come Monday when they were forced to work together.

He pulled her against him, grinding his erection against her backside, and when she still wouldn't give in, he shoved his hands up under her sweater. He freed her from the lace cups of her bra, and as he palmed her bare breasts, she lost it. She moaned and slid her hands up, hooking them around his neck, pulling his head down for a hot and hungry kiss. He yanked the hem of her miniskirt up her thighs, growling when he saw her bare bottom and realized she wasn't wearing panties.

"I didn't have a clean pair," she said, which they both knew was a lie.

"Sure you didn't." He slipped a hand between her

thighs, watching her in the mirror as he stroked, as her cheeks flushed a deep crimson. "Still want me to stop?"

She clearly had lost the will to fight, grinding her ass against the front of his jeans. "Make it fast, before someone realizes we both disappeared."

He unfastened his pants, pulled out the condom he'd put in his pocket and rolled it on. He bent her over the vanity, grabbed her hips and slammed into her. She cried out and bucked her head back, bracing her hands on the vanity edge, meeting him thrust for thrust. Never before had he been so rough with a woman. In his mind women were soft, delicate creatures who required the utmost sensitivity. But with Carrie…he didn't even know how to put it into words. He wanted to dominate her and…*take* her. Make her scream in ecstasy, surrender her body and her mind to him. Her soul. And the more she resisted, the more determined he was to break her.

Their difference in height was making his calves cramp up and throwing off his concentration. He turned Carrie around to face him, lifted her up off her feet and pinned her against the wall next to the shower. Her legs clamped around his hips, nails dug into his shoulders as he thrust inside of her. She murmured encouragement, words like "harder" and "faster," and a few others that he would never use in mixed company. She let him know exactly what she wanted, and how she wanted it. And he couldn't stop now if his life depended on it. Some repressed, primal need had taken over, was driving him past the boundaries of decency. He wanted to put his hands all over her, make her writhe and scream and beg him for more. He'd been with his share of women, yet until that night in her hotel room, he'd had no idea that sex could be so intensely erotic. That he could not just want a woman, but *need* her. In a way that was so primal even he didn't understand it. For a man who thrived on staying in control, being trapped under the spell of a woman, especially one as independent as Carrie, was a place he had never imagined himself. And as hard as he tried he couldn't seem to fight it.

Hell, he wasn't even sure that he *wanted* to anymore.

When he had reached the absolute limit of his control, as sweet release pulled tight in his groin, Carrie smothered a moan against his shoulder and shuddered in his arms, her body clamping around him like a vise, milking him into ecstasy. His orgasm was so intense and draining, his legs so shaky afterward, he had to set her down for fear of dropping her on the hard tile floor.

They were both sweaty and breathless, and crimson blotches stained Carrie's cheeks.

"What is the matter with us?" Carrie said in a harsh whisper, tugging her skirt back down. "We just had sex in your cousin's *bathroom*."

"I know," he said, cleaning up before he zipped himself back into his pants.

Carrie adjusted her bra, tugging the cups back into place. "And you don't see anything wrong with that?"

"I'm just as baffled by this as you are," he said, tucking his shirt in.

"So what are we going to do about it?" she demanded, finger-combing her hair, smoothing away the just-had-sex look.

"Well, right now, I'm going to walk back out to the living room. After a minute or two you'll follow me. You'll tell me you aren't feeling well, and ask me if I'll drive you home. I'll roll my eyes and act indignant, then we'll leave and go to your place. And when we get there we're going to do this again, only this time we can make as much noise as we'd like."

She paused to consider that for several seconds, and

must have determined that it was a good plan, because she gave him a not-so-gentle shove toward the door and said, "What are you waiting for? Get out there."

Nine

The most intense sexual experience of Carrie's life was officially over.

Or so she and Rob had established this morning before he went home to get ready for work. And now, as she walked from the cab to the Caroselli building, after spending nearly twenty-four hours together in bed with him, they had to make everyone believe that they were nothing more than coworkers. At first she didn't think it would be a problem, because she didn't even like him—which she couldn't deny was what had made him so appealing. As a rule she didn't date nice guys. In fact, she avoided them like the plague. She dated jerks. Men who treated her like crap.

Rob seemed to have so much "creep" potential, but then everything had changed. Not only could they burn up the sheets together, but she was beginning to suspect that he was a genuinely nice guy. Under normal circumstances she just wouldn't see him again. If he called or texted, she would ignore him until he got the hint and gave up. That wouldn't be so easy with Rob. Not when she had to interact with him daily, five days a week or more, for the next three months.

He'd even offered to pick her up and drive her to work, because it was on his way, and she'd had to gently remind him that they couldn't be seen together outside of the office. She'd taken a cab instead, and planned, during her first free moment, to arrange for a rental or short-term lease. And because she was a novice at driving in the snow, preferably something four-wheel drive and built like a tank.

Dennis nodded and smiled as she walked past him to the elevator and pushed the button for the third floor. Feeling just the tiniest bit apprehensive she rode up. When she entered the reception area, Sheila greeted her with a smile and said, "Rob would like to see you first thing."

"Thanks," she said, returning the smile. Did Rob not realize that until he gave her a place to work, she had nowhere to go but his office?

She walked down the hall and stepped inside his outer office, where a stern-looking secretary sat. She glanced up from her computer, gave Carrie a quick once-over and seemed to determine that she didn't like her—or so her sour expression would imply. "Go on in, he's expecting you."

Definite tension with this one, which undoubtedly meant that she was loyal to her boss, the one whose work Carrie was here to criticize.

"Thank you, Ms...." Even though the woman's nameplate was in plain sight on her desk, it didn't hurt to break the ice.

"*Mrs*. White," she said, icicles dripping off each word. Ignoring her frosty introduction, Carrie smiled. "It's a pleasure to meet you, Mrs. White. I'm Caroline Taylor, but everyone calls me Carrie."

"Ms. Taylor," she said with a curt nod.

This one would be a tough egg to crack, but Carrie would do it. She had a way of putting people at ease, winning them over. Look how well it had worked on Rob.

A little *too* well.

Only as she approached his office door was Carrie hit with a sudden and intense wave of apprehension. Which was silly given their history. Or maybe what she was really feeling was exhilaration. She could barely go five minutes without thinking of him, without recalling the way he touched her, how he looked tangled in the sheets, ripples of muscles under smooth, sweat-soaked skin.

But it was over now and she would just have to learn to rein in her wandering thoughts.

Steeling herself, she knocked sharply on the door, then let herself in, melting when she saw Rob sitting there, tapping away at his keyboard, a steaming cup of coffee beside him on his desk.

"You asked to see me?" she said, catching the subtle scent of his aftershave, wishing she could run her hand over his smooth, freshly shaved cheek. Even though she couldn't deny that the rasp of the dark, wiry stubble he'd woken up with this morning had been a turn-on.

Without looking up, he nodded and said, "Be with you in just one second.…"

She stood waiting while he typed a bit more, manipulated the mouse for several seconds, frowned, then started typing again. All she could see was the back of the computer monitor, so she had no clue what he might be working on. Or if it even was work. For all she knew he could have been updating his status on Facebook, or corresponding with his online sweetheart. Even though he swore he didn't have a girlfriend. Maybe this would be easier if he did.

While she waited she gazed around his office, which she hadn't really taken the time to notice the last time she was there. In her own defense, it was tough to concentrate on the decor when Rob's hand was up her skirt.

The room was neat, with an unmistakable masculine feel, but not so macho that she had the urge to stuff a wad of chewing tobacco in her cheek. The dark mahogany furniture gave the space a rich, professional feel, but a collection of family photos hanging on the wall and various live plants created a casual atmosphere.

When Rob finally seemed satisfied with what he'd typed, he pushed the keyboard tray in, rose to his feet and greeted her with a very professional "Good morning."

"Sorry I wasn't here sooner. The cab was late picking me up." She waited for him to say something about how, if she'd accepted a ride from him, she wouldn't be late.

He didn't. He just shrugged and said, "No problem."

"What's on the agenda this morning?" she asked, eager to get to work, to keep her mind busy on other things.

"We have a meeting in the conference room in five minutes." He eyed the coat draped over her arm and the briefcase slung over her shoulder. "Why don't I show you to your office first."

He led her down the hall toward the conference room, the scent of his aftershave intoxicating, the casual confidence in his movements mesmerizing. She imagined that once they were in her office he would close the door and pull her into his arms. He would kiss her and tell her that he couldn't keep his hands off her, that he couldn't live without her and that he would die if he couldn't have her again.

When they reached the end of the hall, he hung a left

and gestured to the first office on the right-hand side. "Here it is."

Not only did he not pull her into his arms, but he also didn't even step into the room with her. He waited in the hall while she looked around.

"Will it suffice?" he asked.

It was about half the size of Rob's office and generically outfitted with a desk, bookcase and metal file cabinet. The walls were white and bare, and the carpet an office-gray Berber. Nothing special but functional. "It'll do just fine."

"Great. While you settle in I'll be in the conference room."

He started to turn and before she knew what she was doing, she heard herself say, "Rob, wait."

He turned back to her. "Yes?"

Okay, now what? She wanted to say something, she just didn't know what, or if she even should.

He was standing there, waiting patiently for her to continue, so she blurted out, "I'll need a few things, like Wi-Fi passwords, and I'll need access to a printer."

"We'll discuss all of that in the conference room." He paused, then said, "Anything else?"

Yes, there was something else, she just didn't know how to put it into words. Not without making herself look clingy and pathetic. She forced a smile and shook her head. "No, nothing."

"Then I'll see you down there."

Feeling disappointed for no good reason, she hung her coat on a hook behind the door and stowed her purse in the bottom drawer of her desk. She would need everything in her briefcase for the meeting, so she held on to it.

She had never before questioned her ability to do her job, but as she walked down the hall alone to the conference room, nerves jabbed away at her confidence. Maybe it was the complicated nature of her relationship with Rob that was getting in the way. Yes, they had ended their sexual relationship, but there were still feelings there. It would take time for them to go away completely. And maybe it was a little late to consider this, but what if the past few days hadn't been about sexual attraction as much as his using her to learn her weaknesses? Maybe he would use that information against her to discredit her in front of the people in his department.

Maybe all the while that she had been gushing over what a nice guy he was, it had been an act to lull her into a false sense of security.

A possibility she probably should have considered before she surrendered to him body and soul.

She stopped just outside the conference room door, suddenly convinced she had made a horrible mistake. That by letting her emotions get the best of her, she was about to walk into her worst nightmare. It was imperative that no matter what, she not let anyone see the pain that such a betrayal would cause her.

Taking a deep breath, she stepped into the conference room, head held high, shoulders squared. Rob and three other people sat around the conference table. Her first surprise was that he wasn't sitting at the head of the table, where she would have expected him to be. Her second was that she was greeted with smiles and not scowls when Rob said, "Everyone, this is Caroline Taylor. Over the next three months I expect you to give her your full cooperation."

Huh?

Full cooperation? He wasn't going to give her a hard time? Make her feel unwelcome as he had last week? He was actually going to be nice about this? And why did it suddenly make him about a million times *more* appealing.

Now she was thinking that it would be better if he'd been a jerk. But it was still early. He still had time to knock off some rude or scathing comments. Hell, he had three whole months to prove what a creep he really was. Maybe she had just seen him on his best behavior.

He introduced his team—Alexandra "call me Al" Lujack, Will Cooper and Grant Kelley. They each looked to be in their mid to late twenties and couldn't have been more than a few years out of college.

"Have a seat," Rob said, gesturing to the head of the table, surrendering his authority to her. Crap, he was even nicer than she thought.

She chose the chair beside Al instead and pulled what she needed from her case. "First, I'd like to say that I'm very happy to be here, and I'm looking forward to working with all of you. I want everyone to know it's not my intention to come in and take over the department or diminish anyone's authority. I believe that teamwork is the only way to accomplish goals, and that means I like to hear ideas from everyone. The first six to eight weeks we'll spend analyzing the data, longer if we have to, then we'll discuss our findings, and together outline a viable plan. Does that work for everyone?"

Looking skeptical, Grant asked, "Will it really take that long?"

"It will if we're thorough, and bear in mind we'll be going back twenty years."

There were looks of surprise all around.

"Why so far?" Al asked. "Wouldn't data that old be irrelevant?"

"Not at all. There are many factors we need to consider, and I don't want to risk missing a thing. This will explain my methods." She passed around the folders she had created, outlining all the data they would need and why.

Several minutes passed as they reviewed the material, and Grant said, "As deep as you're digging, compiling data that old could be tricky."

"I have complete faith in everyone."

"As do I," Rob added, going to bat for her once again.

They spent the rest of the day in the conference room, calling in for lunch. She hadn't exactly been sure what kind of leader Rob would be, but from what she could tell so far, he was firm but fair, and it was obvious that his employees respected him. And while they may not have trusted her, they definitely trusted him. And he seemed to, if not trust her, be giving her the benefit of the doubt.

The meeting broke up at six, and everyone went home, or so Carrie assumed. She planned to work only another hour or so, then head home, but when she checked the time later, it was nearly eight-thirty.

"Planning on staying all night?"

Startled, she looked up to find Rob leaning in her office doorway, jacket off, tie loosened, looking too darn yummy for his own good. The dark shadow of stubble across his jaw gave him that I'm-too-sexy-for-my-suit look.

There probably wasn't anyone left in the building....

Carrie, don't even go there.

"I thought everyone had left for the night," Carrie said, and Rob struggled to keep his gaze above her neck, and not on the pillows of cleavage pushing against the form-fitting nylon top she wore under the suit jacket that was now hanging on the back of her chair. Her suit was another story altogether. Unlike last week's shapeless, unflattering garment, this one had a fitted jacket with a tapered waist, and a hip-hugging skirt that reached only midthigh. Her hair was up, but this time it looked looser and sexier somehow. Or maybe it was the same and he was seeing her differently now.

She managed to look both professional and sexy as hell.

It had been torture, not to mention distracting, but he'd managed to keep his hands and eyes off her all day. Well, maybe not his eyes, not completely, but he was careful not to be too obvious.

"I'm here until eight or nine most nights," Rob told her.

"No wonder you don't have a girlfriend," she said, closing her laptop.

That was part of the reason. A fairly large part, actually. "I'm heading home and I thought you might like a ride. No one is here to see us in my car together. Unless that's not the real reason you turned down a ride this morning."

"Of course it's the reason," she said, looking indignant. "What other reason would there be?"

He shrugged. That was the million-dollar question.

She had insisted that they end their affair, that it was the only way to keep a civilized work environment, and claimed she would have no problem with pesky residual feelings. Because while she admitted that they were incredibly good in bed together, she still didn't "like" him. But when he'd asked how she could sleep with someone whom she didn't even like, she'd admitted that she didn't actually dislike him either. He had the feeling that she liked him more than she was letting on.

He could honestly say that he had never met anyone quite like her. And because they had such an intense sexual attraction, and neither was looking for any kind of commitment that extended past the bedroom door, he didn't see the harm in continuing to fool around the full three months that she was here, or at least until they grew tired of each other. But he was honoring her wishes and keeping his distance. For the most part.

"If there is no other reason, then you have no reason to say no to a ride home," he said, and he could see that he had her.

"I guess that would be okay, as long as it's just a ride."

He shrugged. "What else would it be?"

She gave him that look, like he knew damn well.

If someone would be making a move tonight, or any other night, she could rest easy that it wouldn't be him. When he was through with her, she would be begging for it.

"In that case, I'll meet you by the elevator in ten minutes."

"Make it fifteen," he said, just to be difficult. Even he had to have a little fun.

"Fine, fifteen," she agreed, looking exasperated.

Rob went back to his office and finished up a few things, and about twenty minutes later walked to the elevator. She was already standing there waiting, but to her credit she didn't point out that he was late, though he could tell that she wanted to. She had no idea just how easy it would be to ruffle her feathers.

They rode the elevator to the garage, and as the doors opened they stepped off into a wall of icy-cold air.

She shivered under her heavy coat. "I don't think I'll ever get used to this cold."

"Try wearing a hat," he said. "And invest in a well-insulated pair of boots."

"I might just try that," she said, hurrying along beside him to his car. Which was hard to miss being the only one in the lot.

"What happened to the Mercedes?" she asked, as they approached his Escalade.

"They were calling for snow today. This handles better."

When they buckled in with the engine running and the seats warming, she told him, "I wanted to say thank you. For today."

"No problem." He pulled the SUV around to the parking garage entrance and lowered his window to swipe his key card and open the security gate. As he pulled onto the street, he asked her, "Out of curiosity, what did I do today?"

"You showed acceptance when I walked into the conference room, and displayed confidence in me. In doing so, the team will be that much more likely to work well together. It was a nice thing to do."

"I didn't do it to be nice," he said. Mostly he just did it to get laid. He wouldn't seal the deal again by making her life hell.

"Whether you meant it or not, you were."

"I'm still not convinced that just isn't a big waste of time and money. Your methods—"

"Have never failed me before. Just ask my previous clients."

"However," he continued, "you're here, and you're obviously not leaving until the job is done, so there's no good reason not to cooperate." And after going over her plan today, he was slightly less skeptical than he'd been before. Not to mention that now that he really knew her, he couldn't work up the will to disrespect her in front of his team. It just didn't seem right.

"To be honest, it's a bit annoying," she said.

"What's annoying?"

"Your niceness."

"I could act like an ass if it would make you happy."

"That's the thing, I don't think you know how to not be nice."

"And that's annoying?"

"A bit."

There was no doubt about it, Carrie was in a class all by herself.

Ten

Rob glanced over at Carrie, wearing a look that suggested she was just slightly left of center. Or maybe a little more than slightly.

"So, you prefer men who aren't nice?" he said.

"I didn't say that. I just said your niceness is annoying. It's probably that I'm not used to it. I date a lot of jerks."

"And you do this, why?"

She shrugged. "I just do. They're the kind of man I naturally attract. It's an inherited trait. With the exception of my biological father, my mom had lousy taste in men, and so did her mom."

"Why do you think that is?"

"I'm sure the drinking hasn't helped. Although my grandma has been sober since I was little."

"And your mom?"

"She drinks every day. My real dad was killed in the Gulf War, which was when my mom started really drinking. As much as I love her, she was always very fragile. When she lost my dad, she just couldn't handle it. We ended up moving in with my grandma because my mom couldn't pull herself together. She would go to the bar after dinner, stay out until closing, sleep until I got home from school, then after dinner it was back to the bar. It was like that until she met my stepfather, Ben. He was older than her, with an ex-wife and two grown kids in Arizona."

"And he was a jerk?" Rob asked.

"At first he was a godsend. He took care of my mom, and he paid attention to me. He took me to movies and out for ice cream and he would help me with my schoolwork. They were together for only a month when we moved in with him. That was when things started to change."

"I'm assuming for the worse."

"He was an alcoholic, too, but a functioning one. He only drank after work and on the weekends, but when he did drink, he drank a lot. And he was a mean drunk. I learned just how mean the first time I mouthed off to him."

"What did he do?"

"Cracked me across the mouth."

Rob glanced over at her. "He *hit* you?"

"It was backhanded, and only hard enough so that it stung. But as I'm sure you've noticed, I'm not the kind of person who keeps her opinions to herself, so it happened a lot."

"Didn't your mom stop him?"

"She tried once, but he got so mad that she never said anything again."

"Did he hit her, too?"

"There was no need. She did whatever he asked, never argued. I guess in that respect she was the perfect wife."

His grip seemed to tighten on the steering wheel. "Did you tell your grandmother?"

"No way. She was so relieved when Ben came along. She was sick a lot of the time and she didn't have the energy or the patience to take care of my mom. She thought Ben was an angel sent down from heaven. I knew that if I told her what he was really like she would worry. I figured I could handle him on my own. And I did for the most part. My mouth did get me in trouble with my teachers occasionally, but I was an excellent student. It was my ticket out."

"So you stayed there until you graduated?"

"Not quite. When I was sixteen he and I got into a huge fight. I came home three hours past curfew on a school night and he met me at the door."

His brow furrowed, as if he were expecting something unpleasant. "And?"

"Words were exchanged, my mouth got away from me as usual, and I won't deny that I said some pretty horrible things. Nothing that wasn't true, though. He came unglued. He slapped me that time, his full palm against my cheek. It rattled my brain and split my lip and left a bruise the shape of his hand on my face.

"I told him I was going to call the police. He knew he'd crossed the line, so he jumped in his car and took off. He was gone all night. The police showed up around 6:00 a.m. to let us know that he'd been in an accident. He hit a tree and died instantly. There was an open booze bottle in the car, so they assumed it was a DUI, but after the autopsy they discovered that he'd had a heart attack. And he had advanced cirrhosis. He would have been dead in a couple of years anyway."

"How did your mom take it?"

"Surprisingly well. The half-million-dollar insurance payout helped. Plus he had another fifty thousand in investments. She sold the house, bought a condo close to the beach. As far as I know, she's happy."

He shot her another glance. "As far as you know?"

"As you can imagine, there's a fair amount of resentment there on my part, and me being me, I have a tough time putting a filter on it, so when we do talk she walks away from it feeling guilty, which just makes her drink more. Which makes me feel bad. We're both better off if we don't talk often, and when we do, we keep the conversations short. It's not an ideal situation, but it works for us."

"I couldn't imagine not talking to at least one of my parents every day," Rob said, stopping at a red light. "But I guess that comes with being a part of a family business."

"How long have you worked for Caroselli Chocolate?"

"Since birth practically. But I wasn't officially hired until I was thirteen and I started working part-time in one of the stores. When I graduated from college I moved to the main office."

"What did you do then?"

"I started out in the mail room, then worked my way up to the marketing department."

That surprised her. "You had a marketing degree and they started you in the *mail room?*"

"Everyone in the family pays their dues. There's no special treatment and it's very competitive. That includes salary. I could leave the company and go to a marketing firm and almost double my salary. I make most of my money in profit sharing."

"Is there anyone in your family who doesn't work for Caroselli Chocolate?"

Rob pulled down her street. "Tony's sister Christine is mostly a stay-at-home mom. Same thing with Nick's sister Jessica, but they both help out in the stores when they're short-staffed, or around the chocolate holidays."

"Christmas, Thanksgiving, Halloween, Easter and Valentine's Day," she said.

"Very good."

She smiled smugly. "I do my homework. You would be stunned by how much I know about the chocolate industry."

Rob swung the SUV into the driveway, and right away Carrie noticed that something was off. It took several seconds to realize what it was.

"The light is on in the living room."

Rob peered through the windshield to the front of the condo. "So it is. Do you keep it on a timer?"

"No. And it wasn't on when I left this morning."

"Are you sure?"

"Of course I'm sure." First she couldn't close a door, now she was incapable of remembering if she left a light on? Or was she reading way too much into every little thing he said, trying to make him into a bad guy even if he really wasn't? And if so, what did that mean?

Nothing very good, she was pretty sure about that.

She pulled the garage door opener out of her purse. "I planned to go in through the garage, so I left the kitchen light on."

"Maybe the ghost turned it on," he said, and she shot him a scathing look. He shrugged. "Or maybe not."

"I know you think you're funny, but you're not."

Opening doors was one thing, but lights that turned themselves on? It was more likely a burglar than anything supernatural…which was even worse now that she thought about it.

She hit the button for the garage door opener, thinking that whoever it was, if they heard it, would come flying out the front door.

No one did. Still, she was uneasy about just waltzing inside. What if someone was in there waiting for her? Someone too stupid to shut off the light that would alert her to his presence. Just because he was stupid didn't mean he wasn't dangerous.

"You look worried," Rob said.

"Wouldn't you be?"

"Not if I had a poltergeist living in my basement."

She didn't justify that one with a verbal response, but her eye roll said it all.

"You want me to come inside with you just in case?"

She hesitated. The last thing she wanted was Rob, with his sexy stubble, smoldering eyes and ripped muscles, coming into her house and oozing sex appeal all over the place. Sure, he'd been a perfect gentleman all day, but what if he suddenly decided that the platonic arrangement wasn't working for him and he made a move on her?

And suppose there was a deranged psycho in her house waiting to chop her into little pieces and feed her to his pet python? Or make a coat out of her flesh? Which was worse? Death and mutilation or really good sex she shouldn't be having?

Wow, that was a tough one.

"Would you mind?" she asked. "Just in case."

"If I minded I wouldn't have asked. Although if there really was someone in there, hearing the garage door opening probably would have scared them off."

"I'm not sure that's a chance I'm willing to take."

"Let's go." He shut off the engine and they both got out. "Let me go in first," he said as they walked through the garage. To do otherwise would sort of defeat the purpose of asking him in, but she followed close behind him, stopping just shy of clinging to the back of his black wool coat. So close that when he stopped just before the door, she nearly ran into him.

"Key?" he said, holding out his hand.

"Oh, right." She dug through her purse and pulled it out.

She grabbed her phone, too, just in case she had to make a quick call to 9-1-1.

He unlocked the door and pushed it open. The kitchen light was on, just as she had left it, and of course the basement door was open. She followed Rob inside, closing it as she walked past. For all the good it would do. The next time she walked back here it would probably be open again.

As they stepped into the kitchen, the first thing she noticed was the open, half-empty bottle of wine on the counter.

"Did you leave that there?" he asked.

"Why yes, I always have a glass of wine with my breakfast."

He was the one giving the look this time.

"When I left this morning it was in the refrigerator."

He pulled off one leather glove and touched the bottle. "It's still cold."

Who would break into her house and drink a glass of wine?

"I don't suppose you've started smoking," he said.

"No, why?"

He pointed to the kitchen table, where a pack of cigarettes and an old, beat-up silver Zippo lighter lay. She hadn't seen that particular lighter in something like eight years. She gave a sigh of relief to know that they weren't in any imminent danger. At least he wasn't. But Carrie had the feeling she was in for the lecture of her life.

"Alice!" Carrie shouted. "Get in here."

Alice?

Rob looked over at Carrie. Who the hell was Alice?

Before he could ask, a woman appeared in the kitchen doorway. She was nearly as tall as Rob and thin to the point of being gaunt. Silky, pin-straight, jet-black hair framed a face that was as long and thin as the rest of her. She was more striking than beautiful, the kind of woman who would stand out in a crowd.

Dynamic.

"Rob, this is my best friend, Alice," Carrie said. He recalled her mentioning a friend of that name when they were at the diner. He didn't realize that she lived in Chicago.

"Rob?" Alice said, looking him up and down, her crimson lips curling into a slightly lopsided, wry smile. "As in Rob Caroselli, aka Mr. New Year's Eve?"

"The one and only," he said, noticing, as she stepped over to offer him a delicate yet long-fingered hand to shake, she seemed to be walking with a slight limp. She wore black leggings and a long black tunic top. Even her shoes, well-worn ballet flats, were black.

"What are you doing here?" Carrie asked her.

"I haven't been able to reach you in days and assumed you were up to something, which—" she looked pointedly at Rob "—clearly you are."

"He just gave me a ride home. I haven't had a chance to lease a car yet."

Skepticism narrowed Alice's eyes, which were slightly turned up in the corners and an unearthly shade of violet. "Does he always walk you inside?"

"We thought someone had broken in! And by the way, how *did* you get in?"

"How long have we known each other?" Alice said. "You always keep a spare near the front door. It was just a matter of finding it."

Rob looked at Carrie. "You keep a spare key by the *front door?*"

She shook her head and said, "Not now, please."

Alice folded her long, skinny arms under her nearly nonexistent breasts. "You *promised.*"

Promised what? Rob wondered.

"I see you're smoking again," Carrie shot back.

Nice deflection.

"I got *dumped*," Alice said. "What's your excuse?"

Whatever Alice was referring to, it would seem that Carrie had no excuse. Or she couldn't think of one just then.

"That's what I thought," Alice said. "You clearly need supervision."

"It's over," Carrie said, then looked up at Rob. "Tell her it's over."

He looked from one woman to the other, and though he had a pretty good idea of what she meant, he said, "I decline to answer on the grounds that it might incriminate me."

"Did Rex really dump you?" Carrie asked her.

Alice tossed her satiny black hair. "I guess I should have seen it coming. He was never home. And when he was, he was never really there. When I told him that my runway career is officially over, he must have figured the gravy train was drying up for good."

"What do you mean it's over?" Carrie asked, setting her purse and briefcase on the kitchen table. "I thought you just needed time to heal."

"I may have been overly optimistic when I told you that. They said there was a slight chance I wouldn't get full mobility back. But the physical therapy isn't helping and my doctor thinks I might need *another* surgery."

"Oh, honey," Carrie said, shrugging out of her coat. "I'm so sorry."

"I can still do face, or some catalog work, as long as I'm not on my feet for too long or I get a cankle on the left side."

Carrie turned to Rob. "Alice is a very successful run-way model."

"Was," Alice said.

"How long will you be staying?" Carrie asked her.

"I guess it just depends on how long you want me around."

"Stay as long as you like. I can easily turn the office into a bedroom."

"You don't have to do that. I'm perfectly comfortable on the couch. It will be like we're in college again," Alice said, trying to sound cheerful, but her smile looked stiff and forced. Then she looked Rob up and down and added, "Are we going to do the hair band again?"

Rob blinked. "*Do* the hair band?"

"When we were roommates in college we had a system," Carrie explained. "If one of us brought a guy home, we would loop a hair band around the door."

"Oh, like a band for your hair," he said. "That makes more sense."

"Than what?"

He shook his head. "Never mind."

Even if there were any '80s hair bands left, those guys would be ancient by now.

"There won't be a need for the hair band because as I said, it's over." Carrie turned to him. "Would you please tell her that it's over?"

"So you brought guys back to your room a lot in college?"

Carrie rolled her eyes. "Ugh! You're no help."

"I don't know," Alice said, looking him up and down again. "Now that I see him, maybe you should sleep with him again. You could do a lot worse."

"True," Carrie said, giving him the same critical once-over in a way that made him feel a lot like a slab of meat. "But he's kind of…well…*nice*."

Alice's horrified look said she had the same distorted ideas about men that Carrie did. "Never mind."

"On that note, I'm going to go…I don't know…mistreat a kitten or something," he said. "Alice, it was a pleasure to meet you. Carrie, I'll see you at work tomorrow."

"Thanks for coming in with me," she said, walking him to the garage. He recalled specifically that she had closed the basement door on the way in, yet it stood open again.

"It was no problem. Are you sure I can't pick you up on my way in tomorrow?"

"I'm good, thanks."

He wanted to kiss her goodbye, but he didn't. Even though he was pretty sure she wouldn't object. But she was going to come to him this time. And when she was ready, she would. He just had to be patient.

He did know one thing for sure as he got in his car and headed for home: having someone like Alice around was going to be very interesting.

Eleven

On her way down to the break room for coffee, Carrie had to pass Rob's office, and though she had promised herself she wasn't going to go out of her way to see him unless it was completely necessary, it seemed rude not to stop in and thank him for walking her into her condo last night.

So instead of going straight down the hall, she hung a sharp right and stepped into the outer office where Mrs. White sat. Only it wasn't Mrs. White sitting there today. This woman was much younger—in her mid to late forties—and very beautiful. She wore her pale blond hair shoulder-length and pulled back from her face. She was sitting down, but Carrie could see by the long, slender legs encased in cream-colored wool pants that she was tall. *Elegant* was the first word that came to mind.

Maybe Mrs. White was out sick and she was a temp from another department.

"I'm looking for Rob," Carrie told her.

"That makes two of us," the woman said, in a husky voice with a slightly watered-down French accent. "Shall we fight over him?"

Carrie blinked. Fight over... Was she joking? Who did she think Carrie was?

The desk phone rang and Carrie waited for her to answer, but she ignored it. Probably not a temp.

"I just needed to talk to him for a second," Carrie said. "I can come back."

"You're Caroline Taylor?" the woman said.

"That's right." *And who are you?* she wanted to say. She was stunningly beautiful. For all Carrie knew, Rob had a thing for older women.

"I've heard so much about you. From Robby and his father. You're here to save the company?"

"I'm certainly going to try." Unsure of what else to say, she told the woman, "When you see Rob, can you tell him...you know, never mind. It wasn't important."

"I was only teasing you. He is with his father. He should be back any minute." She gestured to the chair opposite the desk. "Sit, wait with me."

Before she could decide to stay or leave, Rob walked in.

He looked from the blonde woman to Carrie and said, "Oh, hi. I see you two have met."

"Well, we didn't actually—"

"Is your father ready?" the woman asked him.

"He said to give him a few more minutes."

"Always a few more minutes," she said with a sigh, telling Carrie, "Husbands, they *always* make you wait."

Husbands? If Demitrio was her husband, that meant she had to be Rob's mother. Carrie never imagined that a woman so fair could give birth to such a dark child. Rob clearly favored his father's side of the family.

"I'm sorry, did you need something?" Rob asked Carrie.

"No."

Then why are you here? his look said.

"I just wanted to talk to you for a second. It's nothing that can't wait." In fact, she never should have come to his office in the first place.

"You two talk," Rob's mother said. "I think I will go see if I can pull Robby's father away from his work."

She stood, and Carrie was right. She was tall—barely an inch shorter than her son. It seemed to be about the only family resemblance Carrie could see. And she must have been older than Carrie thought, unless she'd had Rob when she was twelve.

"It was nice to meet you," she said, shaking Carrie's hand. Then she kissed Rob's cheek and sauntered out.

At the risk of sounding like a dope, Carrie said, "Am I correct in assuming that was your mother?"

"She didn't tell you who she was?"

"She just asked me if I wanted to fight over you."

He smiled and shook his head. "She has a bizarre sense of humor."

Carrie had a sudden, terrifying thought. If Rob's mom knew who Carrie was, did she also know what they'd done? "She doesn't know, right?"

"Know what?"

Duh. She lowered her voice to a loud whisper, just in case someone happened to be in the hall. "About New Year's. About you and me."

He looked at her funny. "You honestly think I tell my mom about my sexual conquests?"

"I don't know—hey, wait. A sexual *conquest?* Is that what I was?"

"You know what I mean, and *no,* I didn't tell her anything," he said, looking offended.

"Sorry. I just thought the French were more open about that kind of thing."

Rob sat on the edge of his desk. "She's not from France. She's from Quebec."

"Six of one, half a dozen of the other."

"Whatever. Point is, no, I didn't tell her. I *never* tell her. As far as I know, she thinks I'm still a virgin."

As if. "I'm sure she knows you're not."

He rubbed his hand across the stubble on his cheek. "Did we ever determine why you came to my office? Because I specifically recall your saying that when we're at work we should pretend not to like each other. Did you change your mind? Did you want to *not like me* in here for a while?"

Oh, so tempting…

"It was something work-related," she told him. "But I've completely forgotten what."

He grinned. "I think you just missed me."

"As if," she said, hating that he was right. From now on, no visits to his office unless it really was work-related.

"Well, when you remember what it was, you know where to find me. Or anything else you might need me for."

"Thanks," she said, and oh, did she wish she could take him up on that.

Rob sat at the conference table three days later with Will and Al, waiting for Carrie and Grant so they could discuss the data they had been compiling, thinking about what Carrie and Alice had said about nice guys. He wasn't sure why he found the idea so annoying, but it continued to nag at him.

"Would you two say I'm a nice guy?" he asked Will and Al.

"Sure," Will said.

"Eh." Al shrugged. "You're okay."

He shot her a look.

She grinned and said, "I'm kidding. Of course you're a nice guy."

"Under what circumstances would you consider that a bad thing?"

Looking confused, Al asked, "Why would that ever be a bad thing?"

"That's what I was wondering," Rob said. "Why would a woman prefer to date a jerk over a nice guy?"

"Does this have something to do with Carrie?" Will asked.

Rob blinked. "Why would you think that?"

"Because of your affair."

"Will!" Al said, giving him a shove.

When Rob got over the shock of his statement, which took a good thirty seconds, he said, "Did Nick or Tony say something to you?"

"They didn't have to," Al said apologetically.

"Yeah," Will agreed, "it's kind of obvious."

No way Rob was that transparent. "Obvious how? We hardly say two words to each other."

"Exactly," Will told him.

"I think what Will is trying to say is that you and Carrie try too hard to act like you *don't* like each other. But when you look at each other..."

"What?" Rob demanded.

"*Major* heat."

Before Rob could confirm or deny their suspicions, Grant rushed in, still wearing his coat. "Sorry I'm late. Traffic was hell this morning."

"It's okay," Al said. "Carrie isn't here yet either."

"Actually she walked in right after me, so she should be along any minute." Grant shrugged out of his coat and hung it on the back of his chair. "She probably stopped in her office."

"We were just talking about Rob and Carrie's affair," Will told him, which earned him another shove from his coworker.

"What about it?" Grant asked, taking a seat.

In response to Rob's blink of surprise, Will said, "Like Al told you, *heat*."

If it was so obvious to them, what about everyone else?

"Good morning!" Carrie said, gliding through the door, her usual cheerful self, and everyone went dead silent.

She set her coffee and a folder down on the conference table and took a seat. Then noticing the lack of conversation, she looked around and asked, "Is something wrong?"

No one seemed to know what to say. Including Rob.

So of course he blurted out the absolute worst thing he could under the circumstances. "Apparently everyone here thinks we're having an affair."

Carrie blinked. "Excuse me?"

"It's not just us, Rob," Al said apologetically. "Pretty much everyone thinks so."

"Why would people think that?" Carrie said, sounding equal parts offended and nervous.

"I'm pretty sure you didn't give yourself that hickey on the back of your neck," Will said.

"Will!" Al said, glaring at him.

Carrie slapped a hand over her neck and cut her eyes to Rob, and her look clearly said, *Oh no, you didn't*.

Oh yes, he had. Their last night together. At the time he had no idea that she wore her hair up for work every day, or he would have branded her somewhere slightly less obvious. He hadn't even realized that anyone else had noticed.

"I must have burned myself with the curling iron," Carrie said, using the same lame excuse his sister Megan had in high school, and Rob could see that no one was buying it.

"Even if it weren't for that, Rob's attitude adjustment made it pretty obvious," Will said.

"Attitude adjustment?" Carrie asked him.

"It's no secret that he didn't think your services were required," Will said. "Then suddenly he was all gung ho to have you here. Everyone just put two and two together."

Carrie went stone-still, and a red blush stained her cheeks. Rob knew exactly what Will was getting at. So did Al. She shoved him hard and shot him a look that said, *Are you kidding me?*

Will just shrugged, as if he didn't have a clue what he'd said wrong.

Al rolled her eyes in disgust. "My *brainless* coworker here did not mean to imply that you were trying to win Rob over by sleeping with him," Al said. "Right, Will?"

The color drained from Will's face and he actually looked as if he might be sick. "Oh…God…Carrie, no, that was not what I meant. Not at all."

"Don't worry about it," Carrie told him, but Rob could see that her feelings were hurt, and even worse, her pride had taken a huge hit.

He had been hoping that by getting their suspicions out in the open, he could have made light of the situation. Even passed it off as a joke. He should have kept his damn mouth shut.

"We haven't seen Rob this happy in a long time," Grant said, joining the painful conversation, which Rob had to admit took courage. "We simply assumed, because your presence here was the only thing different in his life, it probably had something to do with you. I sincerely apologize if we were out of line."

"Then let me say, for the record, Rob and I are *not* having an affair." Carrie sounded calm, but there was an undercurrent of anger in her voice that had Rob worrying that she might blow. That or dissolve into tears, which would probably be worse.

"People, could you give us a few minutes," Rob said.

"Absolutely," Al said, and they practically ran from the conference room. Not that Rob could blame them.

He got up and closed the door behind them, and when he turned back to the table, Carrie was on her feet and standing by the window, her gaze on the street below.

"Well," she said, "that was unbelievably humiliating."

"I am so sorry. I shouldn't have said anything."

"No, I'm glad you did. It's always good to know when people are laughing at you behind your back."

"That's not what they were doing."

"Now do you see?" She turned to him, anger leaking into her voice. "Do you understand why I didn't want anyone to know about us?"

"I honestly don't think Will meant it like that. He has the tendency to put his foot in his mouth." In fact, he was the one who had started this stupid conversation.

"Maybe he didn't mean it that time, but you know they all thought it at some point. That's the way it is in business for a successful woman. No one believes you got there on your own merit."

"You are extremely good at what you do, and everyone knows it. They told me that you and I have obvious chemistry, and that's basically how they knew about us."

"Terrific," she said.

"They're right."

"I know they are. And we can't do a damn thing about it."

"I know." If he really cared about her feelings, cared about *her,* he would back off. Which was exactly what he planned to do. Which sucked, because he honestly believed they could have had something really good, if Carrie could just let her guard down. Even if it was only temporary. Or hell, she could have wound up being the mother of his fifteen-million-dollar heir. Even if it had been a possibility, it would never happen now.

"We could still be friends," he said.

"No, we can't, because people will always wonder if it's more than that."

He shrugged. "So what? Does it really matter that much what other people think?"

"To me it does. I know that probably seems silly to you, but I can't help it. I'm a people pleaser. It's in my genetic makeup. I wouldn't expect someone like you to understand."

"Someone like me?"

"You're rich and handsome and successful. And nice. And fantastic in bed. You're the closest thing to a perfect man that I've ever met. Do you have any idea how intimidating that is? And how inferior it makes me feel?"

"That's ridiculous."

"Yes, it is. And I know that, but it's still how I feel."

"No," he said, taking out his wallet. "What I mean is, it's ridiculous to think of me as perfect. I'm not. Not even close."

He pulled out the small stack of photos that he always carried with him, the ones he looked at every time he was tempted to put something unhealthy in his mouth or skip his morning workout. It was a reminder of just how far he'd come, and how much he didn't want to go back to being that unhealthy, pathetic person.

"Here," he said, handing the pictures to her. "This kid is far from perfect."

As she looked through them, Carrie's eyes grew wide

and her mouth forming a perfect O. "Oh, my gosh, is this *you?*"

"Roly Poly Robby. That's what they used to call me."

"You were so…"

"Fat?"

"I was going to say chubby."

"No, for the better part of my childhood, until I started college, I fluctuated between being twenty-five and fifty pounds overweight. I was *fat.*"

"Slow metabolism?"

He laughed. "No, I liked food. I still do. But back then I didn't have much in the way of self-control, and no interest whatsoever in exercising. I was the uncoordinated, unpopular fat kid who got picked on in grade school, and chosen last in gym class. In middle school I learned I could make the other kids laugh with me instead by telling self-deprecating jokes about my weight, which didn't make me any less miserable. But I convinced my friends and my family that I was confident and happy looking the way I did. I pretended not to mind that girls I liked dated my buddies, when with me they were only interested in being *friends.*"

"But you did mind."

"What teenage boy doesn't?"

"Did you ever try to lose the weight?"

"I don't think there was a time when I *wasn't* trying to lose it. There was always some new diet fad to try. I would do okay for a few weeks, drop ten or fifteen pounds, but I always fell back into my old habits and gained it back. I loathed myself for being so weak. It took me a long time to figure out that diets don't work. That I was just setting myself up to fail, and losing the weight meant completely changing my lifestyle. Becoming healthy."

"And look at you. Your body is…amazing. That must make you proud."

"Sure it does. But the work doesn't end when you reach your goal weight. There isn't a day that I don't struggle with it. The pathetic little fat kid is still in there."

"The exterior doesn't change who you are on the inside. That's what matters."

"Tell me honestly, if we had met in high school with me looking the way I did, would you have been the least bit interested in dating me?"

"I told you, I only date jerks. But if I did choose to judge someone based on their looks or their weight, that's my problem, not theirs. And I apologize for judging you, and calling you perfect before I knew the whole story."

"I've been called worse."

"You do realize what a great guy you are, right? And I'm not just talking looks or physique. You're the entire package. Take it from someone who has met her share of creeps. And I would be the luckiest woman in the world to be with you."

"Yet you're not going to be with me."

"The truth is, you deserve better. I would eventually screw it up. I always do. I would hurt you, and I don't want to see that happen."

For a woman so well put together, who seemed to know just what she wanted, her lack of confidence was astonishing. And the last thing he wanted was to be responsible for making her feel even worse than she already did.

"I'll see to it that everyone is set straight about our relationship," he told her. "I don't foresee anyone hassling you about it, but if anyone does, I'll take care of it."

She shook her head. "That will only make matters worse. If there's a problem, I can deal with it myself."

"Whatever you want. Should we call the others back

in so we can get this progress report started? My dad and Uncle Tony would like to see something from us by end of day and I don't want to rock the boat right now."

"This is probably none of my business," she said, "but I sense a definite rift between your dad and your uncle Tony."

"There's always been a bit of animosity between my uncles and my dad, but in the past couple of months…I don't know. Something is up. My dad keeps saying that nothing is wrong, but it's obvious that he and my uncle Tony are at odds."

"Why is there animosity, if you don't mind my asking? I mean, dysfunctional family relationships are kind of my specialty."

"When my dad was a kid, he was the black sheep of the family. The brilliant-but-bored type. He was constantly getting into trouble in school, and then later with the law. My *nonno*—"

"*Nonno?*"

"It's Italian for grandfather."

"Giuseppe?"

He nodded. "He came here from Italy, and he brought with him a lot of old world traditional values. My dad rebelled against them all, and even worse, he wanted nothing to do with the family business. Finally *Nonno* got fed up. When my dad was twenty-five he was arrested after a bar fight and *Nonno* gave him a choice—sit in jail or join the army. He chose the army."

"Tough love."

"The toughest. Though it was a toss-up as to who was tougher, him or *Nonna*."

"Your grandmother?"

He nodded.

"It obviously did your dad some good."

"Definitely. He went to college and graduated top of his class. After that he came to work for Caroselli Chocolate and shot up the ranks. When *Nonno* retired he made my dad CEO, which both his brothers resented. Plus there's always been some added tension between my dad and Tony."

"Why is that?"

"When my dad went into the army, Tony married his girlfriend, Sarah."

"Yikes."

"Yeah. You can't say that my family history isn't colorful."

"I've learned that most are. But as close as your family is, I'm sure everything will work out."

He hoped she was right. Or everything *Nonno* worked for could crumble around them.

Twelve

Carrie loved what she did for a living. As long as she'd been a consultant, there had hardly been a morning when she woke dreading the workday, even though in the past there had been individuals she dreaded working with.

Usually it was the challenge of saving the company that thrilled her. The act of solving the puzzle. But the past couple of weeks she had begun to realize that this time it was more than that. This time it was the people working for the company that she cared about. It really was like a big family, and hard as she had tried to keep her distance, they had sucked her right in.

As coworkers she and Rob got along exceptionally well together. Their management styles were similar, and what differences they did have seemed to complement each other rather than clash. It was as if he could anticipate her next move before she even made it, and they were so in sync that they'd even begun finishing each other's sentences. If ever she had to choose her favorite assignment, hands down this was it. Yet she was torn between loving it, and the fear of getting *too* close.

When Carrie wasn't working, most of her free time was spent with Alice—who wasn't nearly as blasé about her breakup with Rex or her career change as she'd let on. But there were times when she found herself wishing she could be with Rob. Sometimes at work they would stand close to one another and she would get that soul-deep longing to touch him, or he would look at her a certain way and her knees would go weak. She missed the intimacy of their physical relationship—and not just the sex. She missed the way they would lie in bed, side by side, fingers entwined, and just talk. Usually about nothing in particular.

He could be intense at times, and was passionate in his convictions, but his dry wit appealed to her snarky sense of humor. He didn't take crap from her or anyone else, and when someone gave him a hard time he didn't hesitate to call them out on it. He had integrity, and radiated a confidence that was infectious. With a few simple words of praise he could make a person feel as if they were something really special, because while he wasn't a negative boss, he only handed out compliments where they were earned. Which seemed to make his employees strive to please him. Hell, even she felt a little nervous about possibly letting him down, when as a rule she never let herself become emotionally invested in a client. And she typically never formed attachments. But so far, nothing about this job was what she would call typical.

She even began to think that Rob being a nice guy wasn't such a bad thing after all and if there was a man out there who could ever put up with her, he might have actually been it. Which of course scared the living hell out of her. Alice had once accused Carrie of being afraid to be happy, and Carrie was beginning to wonder if maybe she was right. Maybe she was worried that with happiness came the possibility of losing that happiness. It was so much easier to have low expectations, and hurt less when the inevitable letdown came.

Alice used to be her number one supporter when it came to Carrie's hang-ups, but lately she seemed to be defecting to the other side.

"You're an idiot," she said after Carrie hung up from a work-related phone call to Rob that had turned into a two-hour-long conversation that had absolutely nothing to do with marketing reports.

Carrie looked up from the work spread out on the bed. "We've been friends for over ten years and you're just now noticing this?"

"Do you honestly not see how good you two are together? How much he cares about you? And I mean *really* cares. You just talked for two hours. I was lucky if I could get Rex to talk for ten minutes."

"He deserves better than someone like me."

"Isn't that up to him to decide?"

Alice wasn't in any position to be passing judgment. She excelled at snagging emotionally unavailable men. Which always landed her where she was right now. Miserable and alone with shattered self-esteem.

"We're coworkers," Carrie said. "I don't date coworkers."

"You told me yourself how well you guys work together, so that lame excuse is not going to cut it anymore."

"I live in Los Angeles, he lives in Chicago. Talk about a long-distance relationship."

"Other than your mom, who you barely even talk to, what do you really have in Los Angeles that you couldn't have here?"

The answer should have come immediately, and it surprised Carrie to realize that she had no answer. What did she have in Los Angeles, other than work, which frankly she could do anywhere? Her best friend lived all the way across the country, and she worked so much she didn't have time to make other friends. Or at least, that was what she liked to tell herself.

"I'm tired of sleeping on the couch," Alice said out of the blue.

"I told you before that I could turn the office into a bedroom."

"You're not tired of me yet?"

"Of course not. I was sort of hoping that you would stay here with me until I go back to L.A."

"In that case I should probably order some bedroom furniture."

"Renting it would be a lot cheaper."

She sighed. "As much as I love to shop, you're probably right. Until I decide what to do with my life, I should probably watch my spending."

"I'll call Terri tomorrow and make sure it's okay."

"I'll look online for a furniture rental place."

Carrie called Terri from work the next afternoon.

"Of course you can turn the office into a bedroom," Terri said. "Just stick what's in there down in the basement."

"Perfect! Thanks, Terri."

"And by the way, I was going to call you. We're having a get-together next weekend. We would love it if you would come."

And she would love to be there, which was exactly why she shouldn't go. She was letting herself get too close. This was just supposed to be a business trip. "My friend Alice is visiting and I would feel bad leaving her alone."

"Bring her with you."

Terri was making it very hard to say no gracefully. "The thing is, she just got out of a relationship and I'm not sure if she's ready to put herself back out there just yet. But I will ask."

"I hope we see you."

Carrie wished she could.

A few minutes after she hung up with Terri, Alice called. "Did you talk to Terri?"

"She said it's fine, and we can move the furniture that's in there down to the basement."

"I already picked out the furniture. I thought I would have them deliver it Monday. We can move the office furniture tomorrow. Unless you're planning to work again this weekend."

"I think I've earned a Saturday off," she said. It was hard to believe that today would mark the end of her fourth week in Chicago, and her third at Caroselli Chocolate. And they still had so much work to do.

After they hung up Carrie immersed herself in work until Rob appeared in her doorway later. With his sleeves rolled to his elbows and his tie loosened, he looked too yummy for words. She longed to undress him, and run her tongue over every conceivable inch of his delicious body.

"Tony and I are packing it in and going out for a burger," he said. "Care to join us?"

She looked at the clock, surprised that it was already after seven. "I can't."

He folded his arms. "You're not still worried that people will think we're a couple, are you?"

"No, not anymore." Everyone seemed fairly clear on that concept now. Though it wouldn't take much to get the rumor mill spinning again. If there was one thing the Carosellis loved more than chocolate, it was gossip. "I'm taking the weekend off, so I want to finish this report before I go. It's going to be at least another hour or two."

"You sure? Dinner is on me."

"Maybe next time."

He shrugged. "Okay, see you tomorrow."

"See ya."

He was already long gone when it occurred to her that she wouldn't be there tomorrow, so she in fact would not see him. Which was probably a really good thing. She was very careful to stay safely behind the border she had set for herself. Yet every now and then she caught her toes inching past the line. That was when she knew she had to back off, recapture her perspective.

She worked until nine, and was gathering her things when she swore she heard the sound of footsteps out in the hall. It was rare that anyone worked past six on Friday, and for a split second she wondered if Rob had come back.

She got up from her desk and peeked out of her office, just in time to see someone turn the corner at the end of the hall, where it dead-ended at Demitrio's office. Someone too small to be Rob or any other man.

Had his secretary come back for something maybe?

She walked quietly down the hall and peeked around the corner. Whoever it was, she was messing with the door to the outer office.

What have we here? she wondered. A little interoffice espionage?

"Excuse me," she said and the woman in question squealed with surprise, dropping whatever was in her hand. As it clinked against the granite floor, Carrie realized that it was a large silver paper clip that had been straightened out.

Was she *picking* the lock?

The woman spun around and Carrie recognized her immediately. "Rose?"

"Carrie," she said, slapping a hand over her heart. "You scared me. I thought everyone had left."

Carrie only knew Rose from the break room, and though she found her to be a bit odd, she'd never had a problem with her. But something was definitely going on. "What are you doing?"

Her cheeks blushed bright red as she bent down to grab the paper clip. "I realize how this looks," she said nervously, "but it's not what you think."

"You're picking the lock on the CEO's office door."

"Demitrio's secretary has a binder full of old reports for me that need to be digitized. She left early, but said it would be on the corner of her desk. I lost track of time, and by the time I came down to get it, Demitrio had left and locked up. I tried to reach her, and when I couldn't, I panicked. I thought maybe I could pick the lock."

She looked sincere, so why did Carrie get the feeling she was lying through her teeth. "Would you like me to call Rob? Maybe he has a key to his father's office."

"Oh, wait! My phone is ringing. Excuse me."

Carrie didn't hear a phone ring, but supposed Rose could have had it set on silent.

She scurried several feet away before answering it. "Hello," she said. "Oh, thank goodness you got my messages…are you sure it can wait?" She paused, then said, "Okay, see you Monday." She turned to Carrie, shoving the phone back in her pocket. "It's okay. She said I can do it Monday."

Carrie found it awfully convenient that she called at that exact moment. A little *too* convenient. Not only that, but

Mary, Demitrio's secretary, was a talker. They'd never had a conversation that lasted less than ten minutes.

"Would you mind if we keep this between us?" Rose said, her cheeks crimson. "I would be mortified if anyone knew what I did."

"Sure," Carrie said, fully intending to tell Rob the entire story the next time she saw him.

At noon the next day, when she and Alice were supposed to be moving furniture to the basement, Carrie found her draped on the couch half-asleep instead.

"Are you ready?" Carrie asked her.

"Ready for what?"

"To move the office furniture."

Alice blinked. "With my healing ankle? I couldn't possibly."

"Then why did you tell me you would?"

"I never said *I* would do it personally."

Did she think Carrie would be able to do it alone? "I need help."

"Don't worry." She sat up, stretching like a cat. "I called for reinforcements."

"Reinforcements?" Who did she even know in Chicago? Or had she hired professional movers?

As if on cue, the doorbell rang. Alice put her foot down, wincing as she tried to push herself up from the couch. "Be a dear and get that for me, would you?"

Be a dear?

She walked to the door wondering why Alice was acting so odd. She pulled it open, surprised to find Rob standing there. Tony was behind him.

"We're here," Rob said.

Thanks, Captain Obvious. "I see that. *Why* are you here?"

Confused, the two men looked at each other, then Rob turned back to her. "Alice called. She said you needed help moving furniture."

"Oh, did she?" Carrie turned to give her friend the evil eye, but the sofa was empty. She'd set Carrie up, now she was going to bail on her? How many times had Carrie specifically said that she didn't want to see Rob outside the office?

"Come on in," she said, letting the men inside. She couldn't leave them out in the cold while she murdered Alice. Besides, she really did need their help. They might even lend a hand disposing of Alice's body.

Under his wool coat Rob looked like something out of a handyman fantasy in faded, threadbare blue jeans, a flannel shirt with the sleeves rolled up and well-worn work boots. The kind of ensemble that would be fun to tear off him with her bare hands. Which was exactly what she wanted to do.

Yep, Alice was dead meat.

Wearing black jeans, a black long-sleeved T-shirt and sneakers, Tony wasn't looking too shabby either.

"If you two will excuse me a minute, I need to have a word with my roommate."

"You want us to get started?" Rob asked.

"Nope," she called over her shoulder as she headed down the hall. "I'll be right back."

Her bedroom door was closed, and when she tried to turn the knob, it was locked. She had locked Carrie out of her own bedroom?

"Alice!" she hissed. "Open the door."

"I have a terrible migraine," Alice said weakly. "You'll have to manage without me."

"Migraine, my ass," she mumbled as she walked back to the living room, where Rob and Tony were still waiting.

"Everything all right?" Rob asked.

"Fine. Alice is…resting in my room."

Rob's brow rose. *"Resting?"*

The last thing she wanted was for Rob to realize that this was a setup. He might actually believe that Carrie had something to do with it.

Carrie lowered her voice and said, "Actually, she's hiding. She's taking the breakup pretty hard. And the career stuff."

"Tony is a recent dumpee, too," Rob told Carrie.

"Dude, really?" Tony said, looking irritated. "Tell the whole world, why don't you."

Rob grinned, and Carrie wondered if that had been payback for past fat jokes.

"Alice said you're clearing out the office," Rob said.

"We're making it a bedroom." They followed her down the hall. "So this is it," she said as they stepped into the spare room. "It all has to go. Terri said to put everything in the basement."

"The haunted basement?" Tony said.

She couldn't believe that a big burly guy like him could possibly be afraid of a door-opening spirit. "Whatever or whoever it is down there, it's harmless," Carrie assured him.

Both men took an end of the desk, carried it out of the room and down the hall.

"Where in the basement do you want it?" Rob asked her.

"Oh, anywhere there's room," she said.

"Nowhere specific?"

She shrugged. "Just any old place is fine."

Rob stopped just shy of the basement door, wearing a wry smile. "You've never been down there, have you?"

"Why would you assume that?"

Tony looked down the stairs, then back at her. "Have you?"

"Yes," she said indignantly, then paused and added, "Sort of."

"Sort of, how?" Rob asked.

She'd once made it about halfway down the stairs, but the creak of the door moving behind her had propelled her back up. She'd moved so swiftly, in fact, that she could swear her feet never touched the stairs. "Even if there is something down there, it's not as if it can hurt us."

"Then you won't mind going first," Rob said, gesturing her down.

Unwilling to admit just how nervous she was at the prospect of going down there, she raised her chin a notch, met his challenging gaze and said, "Of course I'll go first."

"We'll be right behind you," Rob said.

She switched on the light and peered down. Worst-case scenario, she might see or hear something unusual. And because whatever kept opening the door seemed inclined to stay in the basement, she had nothing to worry about. Plus she had two strapping men to protect her.

Yet she was still edgy.

She started down, forcing her feet forward, growing colder as she descended, unsure if it was due to a lack of heat or the presence of something unworldly. She was hesitant to hold the rail, lest she might feel that disembodied hand settle over hers again. Her heart was pounding double time when she reached the last step and her foot hit the concrete floor.

She realized, with no small degree of relief, that the only things down there she could see were boxes and old furniture. *Extremely* old furniture and lots of it. Pieces that she was guessing were from the late nineteenth century. It must have been worth a small fortune.

"I guess we should put the stuff from the office off to

the side over there," she said, gesturing to the only relatively vacant area.

They set down the desk and Rob asked, "Are you coming back up with us?"

"I think I'll stay down here," she said, curiosity outweighing her fear.

"Okay, we'll be right back."

She wove her way through the maze of different pieces, checking them out. Some were plain and functional, others ornately embellished and fragile-looking. She knew next to nothing about antique furniture, but the variety of grains and colors said the pieces were built from several different types of wood. Whoever owned all of this must have been a collector.

There were several dining room and bedroom sets, and a fair share of living room pieces. She ran her hand across the surface of a beautifully carved sideboard, expecting to find a layer of dust but either the air in the condo was unprecedentedly clean, or Terri sneaked in while she was at work and dusted everything.

"Find your ghost?" Rob asked as he and Tony appeared with a large file cabinet.

"Not exactly. But doesn't it seem unusually clean down here? There isn't a spot of dust on this furniture."

"Terri is a little fanatical about keeping things clean," Rob reminded her.

Yes, but a basement? Besides, she hadn't been there in a month.

"We just have to grab the bookcase and we'll be done," he said.

"Okay," she answered distractedly, entertaining a third possibility, but it was a little creepy to contemplate that not only was the ghost fanatical about keeping doors open, but it was a clean freak as well. Could a ghost have OCD?

Carrie heard a soft creaking sound, and she could swear the very faint wail of a baby crying.

No way. It must have been something Alice was watching upstairs, and the sound was leaking down through the floorboards.

And what if it wasn't?

"Do you guys hear that?" she said, turning to where Rob had been standing. But apparently they had already gone back up the stairs for the next load.

She listened hard and the sound seemed to be coming from the far end of the basement, where the bedroom pieces were stored. Coincidentally, right under the bedrooms.

Screwing up all of her courage, she made her way through the furniture, following the sound, and the closer she got, the less it sounded as if it were coming from upstairs. She finally made it to the end of the basement, in the darkest corner and found, stored behind a wide chest of drawers that was desperately in need of refinishing, a child's cradle that looked hand-carved. As her eyes adjusted to the low light, and she got a better look at it, the hair on her arms and back of her neck shivered to standing and her heart skipped a beat.

The cradle was rocking.

She blinked, then blinked again, sure that her eyes were playing tricks on her. But it really was rocking. Not only that, but the crying was louder now, as if it were right in front of her. Loud wailing that wasn't really loud at all. It was all around her, but almost as if she were hearing it on the inside of her head. She stood there mesmerized watching it move back and forth, back and forth, and as she did she felt herself reaching out to touch it...then a hand slammed down on her shoulder and a blood-curdling scream ripped from her throat.

Thirteen

"It's just me!" Rob said as Carrie whipped around, losing her balance and falling against the bureau she'd been looking behind.

"Are you trying to give me a heart attack?" she shrieked, giving him a shove.

"I'm sorry," he said, holding his hands up to ward off another attack. "I called your name three times and you didn't answer me. I came back here to see what you were looking at but I tripped on a table leg."

From behind them he heard the thud of footsteps on the stairs, and turned to see Tony descending two steps at a time. Following him by only a few seconds was Alice, who once again was dressed all in black.

"What the hell happened?" Tony and Alice said at the same time, then turned to each other in surprise, as if they had completely missed one another on the stairs.

"Nothing," Rob said. "I just surprised her."

"Surprised me? You scared the crap out of me."

"I told you, I tripped."

"Did you see it?" she demanded.

"See what?"

"The cradle. It was rocking. And I could swear I heard a baby crying."

Uh-oh. Had he scared her so thoroughly that she had lost touch with reality? "What cradle?"

"Back there." She pointed to the spot behind the bureau she'd been staring at when he fell into her.

He peered behind it, and though the light was dim he could definitely see the outline of something small and low to the floor, wedged between the bureau and the wall.

"Is it still rocking?" she asked.

As far as he could tell it wasn't moving. "Let me see if I can…" He leaned over the bureau, his stomach resting on the top, reaching…

He grabbed the side of the cradle and pulled it up off the floor. It was light, and looked to him to be almost small enough to be a child's toy rather than a functional piece of furniture, but as he held it up to the light he could see that it was handmade and very old.

Her concerns suddenly gone, Carrie started making her way back to where Tony and Alice stood, gesturing him to follow. "Bring it over here!"

He had never known Carrie to be anything but level-headed and rational, but she was neither right now.

He held the cradle up over his head and carried it through the maze of furniture. When he reached the other side, where the three of them stood waiting for him, he set it on the cold concrete floor. It was simple but functional, and looked surprisingly well-kept considering its age, but probably not very safe by modern standards.

"Watch it!" Carrie said excitedly. "I swear it was rocking all by itself. And I heard a baby crying."

"A *human* baby?" Rob asked, which Carrie's exasperated look would suggest was a stupid question.

"Of course a human baby," she said. "Didn't anyone else hear it?"

Rob shook his head, and they both turned to Tony and Alice, who were ignoring them and busy giving each other the once-over. Rob realized that they hadn't been introduced yet. "Tony, this is Carrie's friend Alice, from New York. Alice, this is my cousin Tony."

"A pleasure," Alice said, shaking Tony's hand, a catlike grin curling her lips.

"The pleasure is all mine," Tony said, and they looked utterly enthralled by one another.

"How about a drink?" Alice said, her eyes never leaving Tony's.

"I'd love one," Tony said, gesturing to the stairs. "After you."

As they disappeared up the stairs, Carrie turned to Rob and said, "What the heck just happened?"

Rob shrugged. "I guess they liked what they saw."

"In that case, maybe it's a good thing that you made me scream." She looked down at the cradle, which as far as Rob could see, wasn't moving at all. Sounding defeated, she said, "It's not going to do it for you."

"It might."

They stood in silence and watched it for several minutes, but nothing happened.

"I swear it was moving," she told him.

"I believe you. If doors can open by themselves, why would a self-rocking cradle be such a stretch of the imagination?"

"Either that, or I'm losing my mind."

"It *was* a little weird that you wouldn't answer me. At first I thought you were upset about something. And then I thought maybe you were getting sick."

"Eew," she said, nose wrinkling.

"But as I got closer, it seemed as if you were in a trance or something."

"I guess I sort of felt like I was. And when you fell against me, I think I was reaching down to touch it. But I wasn't doing it consciously. Does that make sense?"

"Not really."

"I could see my arm moving, but I didn't feel as if I was controlling it."

"Are you saying that you were possessed?"

She shrugged. "Maybe I was. I sure didn't feel like myself."

If she were anyone else, he would think she was either nuts or looking to get attention, but that wasn't Carrie. She was one of the most down-to-earth, sane people he'd ever met, despite all her hang-ups. A genuine straight shooter. She looked so damn adorable in her skinny jeans and a UCLA sweatshirt, her hair pulled back in a ponytail that bounced when she walked. And he wanted her just as much as he had in the hotel bar that night. He'd racked his brain trying to come up with a way to make her see that she was wrong. He didn't deserve better than her, because there was no one better. Not that he'd ever met. The problem was making her believe that.

"I guess we should get back upstairs," she said.

"You want me to bring the cradle up?"

She looked at all the furniture piled there, then at the forlorn little cradle on the floor. He thought of the children who might have slept in it and actually felt guilty for leaving it down there. It looked so small and lonely.

Small and lonely? Where the hell had that come from? Now *he* was acting possessed.

"Bring it up," she said. "I'll clean it up. Maybe someone can get some use out of it."

He lifted the cradle off the floor, and as he did, he could swear he felt a rush of cold air brush past him. Clearly he was imagining things.

He followed Carrie up the stairs, holding the cradle, and when they stepped through the door, she pushed it closed behind him.

Just before he heard the knob latch, from the basement below, he could swear he heard the sound of not a baby, but a woman crying.

"They bailed on us." Carrie held up the note she found stuck to the refrigerator and showed it to Rob.

Went for a drink. Back later.

"I guess Tony forgot that we came here together in his car," Rob said.

Carrie wasn't thrilled by the idea of being stuck with Rob, and even though it was a setup, she couldn't muster the will to be upset with Alice. She'd been cooped up in the house for three weeks. It would do her good to get out and socialize. She needed this. And maybe she and Tony would hit it off. Alice could certainly benefit from meeting a nice guy for a change. Not that Carrie knew Tony all that well. But if he was anything like the rest of his family, she had nothing to worry about.

She had the sudden vision of her and Alice both settling down in Chicago, and a double wedding with Carrie and Rob and Alice and Tony tying the knot.

A double wedding? Seriously? Where the heck had that come from?

She shook away the ridiculous notion.

"I'm sure they won't be too long," she said. At least she hoped they wouldn't.

"Where do you want the cradle?" Rob said, and she realized he was still holding it.

"The living room, I guess, until I figure out what I'm going to do with it. It just didn't seem right to keep it in the basement."

"I know what you mean," he said, carrying it into the living room for her.

"You do?"

He set it down by the couch, then sat down. "Weirdly enough, yes."

The fact that she'd felt that way was weird, but his feeling it, too? That was downright creepy. Maybe, instead of cleaning it up, she should hire an exorcist.

She sat in the chair. "Do you like old furniture?"

"Not particularly."

Neither did she. She didn't dislike it, but her preference was a more modern look. But the cradle, there was just something about it....

"Maybe that's why the door kept opening," Rob said. "Maybe whatever is down there wanted you to find it and bring it up. Maybe that's why it touched you that first night."

She narrowed her eyes at him. "Are you serious or just making fun of me?"

"I heard it, too," he said.

"The baby crying?"

"Just before you closed the basement door. But it didn't sound like a baby. It was a woman."

The hair on the back of her neck rose. "Wow, that's really creepy."

"I have to admit that it is."

"Speaking of creepy," Carrie said, "something happened at work last night that I thought I should mention."

"Don't tell me doors are opening by themselves there,
too," he said, with a grin so adorable she wanted to eat
him up.

"This is about a door that wouldn't open, actually."

She told him how she had caught Rose trying to break
into his father's office, and how his secretary conveniently
called at the last second.

"You think she was lying?" Rob asked her.

"I'm usually pretty good at reading people, and I definitely had that feeling. But that doesn't mean I'm right. I
just thought I should tell you."

"I'm glad you did. Just between us, there's something
about her that bothers me."

"Me, too! She's so quiet—not that quiet people are
bad—but it always seems as if she's up to no good or hiding something. Do you know what I mean?"

"I do. She and my sister have become pretty good
friends. Megan bought an apartment and Rose is going to
be moving in the end of this month."

"You're worried?"

"Yeah. Her mom worked at Caroselli Chocolate for
years as *Nonno's* secretary, so when she showed up looking for a job, my uncle Leo felt obligated to hire her."

"In what position?"

"At first, just general office stuff, but then she offered
to digitize all our old records, and that's been her job de-
scription ever since."

"So she has access to a lot of company information."

"You think she's a spy?"

She shrugged. "It does happen."

"I think I'll do some digging. See what I can come up
with." He looked at his watch. "If Tony ever comes back."

It was obvious that he didn't feel like hanging around. She didn't know if she should feel relieved or disappointed. "I can drive you home."

"You wouldn't mind?"

"Consider it my thanks for moving the furniture." It beat having him stuck there until God knew when, driving her crazy. "I'll get my coat."

It was snowing lightly as she backed out of the garage. She still wasn't crazy about driving in the snow, but it wasn't half as bad as she'd expected, and the compact SUV she'd leased totally kicked ass.

"Are we supposed to get much snow?" she asked Rob.

"They said something about six inches tonight."

"So," she said, glancing over at him, "average?"

He laughed and shook his head. "That's what I hear."

She could really go for six inches tonight. Or in Rob's case, seven or eight.

What? No! Did she really just think that? She had to get her mind out of the gutter and stop flirting with him. This is why she didn't like to see him outside of work. She forgot how to behave. And being in such a confined space with him, the scent of his aftershave was doing funny things to her head.

It was making her fantasize about things. Bad things, like what he would do if she took her hand off the steering wheel and laid it on his knee, maybe slid it up his inner thigh...

Don't even think about it.

This is why it was such a bad idea to see each other socially. She had no self-control.

"Make a left here," Rob said. "My building is two blocks down."

They couldn't have gone more than half a mile from

her place. "I knew you were close, but I didn't realize it was this close."

"If it wasn't so cold, I would have just walked."

The area was an eclectic blend of old restored and new buildings. Rob's was a converted warehouse. "Beautiful building," she said. "What floor are you on?"

"I have the penthouse."

"Sounds nice."

"It's open concept. Very modern. Want to come up and see it?"

Hell no. "Um…sure."

What? No, you don't!

If she got him alone in his place, she wasn't sure if she could be responsible for her actions. In fact, she knew she couldn't.

"Do you have a roommate?" she asked.

"No, why?"

She shrugged. "Just curious."

She needed to come up with an excuse as to why she couldn't go inside. But as he pointed out a parking space just a little ways down the street, the car seemed to drive itself there.

This was a *really* bad idea. But that didn't stop her from getting out of the car and walking with him to the building. It was as if she was having an out-of-body experience, watching the scene from above but not really participating.

The lobby was clean and modern and even better, toasty warm.

"How long have you lived here?" she asked while they waited for the elevator, hoping that idle conversation would keep her from doing something crazy like throwing herself at him. She'd actually had sex in an elevator before. It wasn't all it was cracked up to be. But with Rob, there was no such thing as bad sex. Or even mediocre sex.

They stepped off the elevator into a hallway with just two doors. He pointed to the one on the right. "This is me."

He unlocked the door and gestured her through, and as she stepped inside, what she saw took her breath away.

When he said open concept he hadn't been kidding. The apartment was one big open space with a gourmet kitchen, a dining space and a cozy living area. A mix of steel and wood beams crisscrossed above their heads, and a winding iron staircase led to a loft-style bedroom. Tall windows that looked original to the building lined one entire side of the unit.

"This is beautiful!" she said.

"Take off your coat."

"Oh…I can't stay."

He shrugged out of his coat and hung it on a hook beside the door. "You in a hurry to be somewhere?"

"Well…no, but—"

"So stay a few minutes." He held his hand out for her coat. "You don't have to worry, I'm not going to put the moves on you."

As if she needed encouragement from him. If anyone was going to be putting moves on, it probably would be her. Knowing that, she slipped off her coat anyway and he hung it beside his own.

"I'll give you the grand tour."

He showed her around, pointing out all the unique, special touches, but she was having trouble concentrating. Her eyes kept wandering to his ass, which looked exceptionally nice in jeans. He had his usual afternoon stubble and she longed to feel the roughness of it against her palms and her lips…maybe her thighs. She kept her hands wedged in the pockets of her jeans so she wouldn't be tempted to use them, and as they climbed the winding stairs to his bedroom, she couldn't help thinking that she was making a huge mistake.

"The bedroom is my favorite room."

She didn't ask why. She didn't want to know, but as they walked to the window, it was obvious.

The view from downstairs was nice, but from up here, it was breathtaking. She could see the entire neighborhood, and in the distance, the skyline of downtown.

"It's amazing," she said, aware that he was standing just a few inches behind her. So close she could feel his body heat and smell his aftershave—or maybe that was just how the room naturally smelled. On an oversize chair beside her lay the clothes that Rob had worn to work yesterday—yes, she paid attention—and she had to fight the urge to pick up his shirt and hold it to her nose, breathe in the scent of his skin on the fabric.

Maybe when he wasn't looking…

"I can lie in bed and watch the fireworks at Navy Pier."

"Nice," she said. She could think of other things they could do in bed, too. They could make their own fireworks.

"Is everything okay?" he said. "You're awfully quiet."

She shrugged. "Not much to say, I guess."

"You always have something to say."

He was right. She didn't like quiet. She was always filling the empty space with conversation. Today was different. Today she was terrified that she would say something she shouldn't, which might encourage him to do something *he* shouldn't. Something she would find it impossible to say no to.

She turned to him, looked up into his dark, bottomless eyes. The longing that she saw there, the unmasked *need,* made her knees go weak.

She never should have turned around.

"I want you," she said, regretting the words the instant they left her lips.

He nodded. "I know."

"But I can't. I can't want you."

"I know that, too."

Did he have to be so damn agreeable?

"The thing is, you're a lot bigger than me," she said. "If you were to grab me and throw me down on the bed, there wouldn't be much I could do to stop you."

"So you have someone else to blame later?" He took a step back. "Not a chance."

She blinked in surprise. He was turning her down?

"This isn't a game," he said. "Not to me, anyway. Not anymore."

"I know that."

"Then you need to make up your mind. Either you want me or you don't."

"I do, but—"

"No buts," he said. "Either we're together or we aren't."

"What about work?"

"Work is work. We keep it professional. It's no one's business what we do outside the office."

No, but they sure liked to make it their business.

"You can't tell anyone. Not even Nick and Tony." She paused and said, "Well, I guess it would be okay to tell them. If they ask. I would never expect you to lie to them. But no one else."

"So I should forget about that announcement I was going to run in the Sunday paper?"

She smiled. He *always* made her smile. He made her... happy. Why would she deprive herself of that? What reason did she have to say no?

Because you like him, dummy. Too much. In her entire life she had never met anyone she would have even considered seeing long term, yet here she was doing crazy things like imagining double weddings. This was a totally new experience for her. It was exciting and terrifying. What if she got too attached? What would she do when it was over? Did she really want to put herself through that?

But what if this time was different? What if there wasn't a letdown? What if there really was someone for everyone, and Rob was her someone? Wouldn't it be worth it to at least find out? To at least give him a chance?

She thought about what Alice said, about what Carrie had to go back to in Los Angeles, and she was right. When Carrie wasn't working, her life was barren and lonely. Here she at least had people who genuinely seemed to care about her.

"I want you," she said.

He looked skeptical. "But?"

She shook her head. "No buts. Not this time."

"You're sure?"

"Very sure." She slid her arms around his neck, rose up on her toes and kissed him.

Fourteen

"Is he in there?" Carrie asked, poking her head into Mrs. White's office.

"He already went down to the conference room," she said, her tone considerably less chilly than it had been eight weeks ago.

No matter how impersonal or cold the older woman was, from day one Carrie had greeted her with a smile and treated her with respect. It had taken a while to realize that she wasn't really a bitch, just very focused and private. And one hell of a good secretary. She liked to come in and do her job and she didn't like to be interrupted, which Carrie could certainly relate to. And she was fiercely loyal to Rob. He told Carrie that when he was a kid she worked in one of the stores and was a totally different person. He said she would always slip him an extra piece of his favorite candy when he came in with his mother to visit. Even if his mother said no more—which was usually the case.

Then Mrs. White's only son was killed in an accident, and she hadn't been the same since.

So Carrie and she would never be pals, or even friends, but their working relationship was now amicable.

"Did he get my report?" she asked Mrs. White.

"He did. He took it with him."

She shouldn't be nervous, but she was. After compiling all the data, Carrie had worked up a rough plan of what she thought was a viable solution to Caroselli Chocolate's sales drop. Now she would present it to the rest of the team and hoped they agreed she was on the right track and were willing to implement a plan. She was especially nervous about what Rob would think. For the past five weeks, since they began officially secretly "dating," they had managed to keep their private and professional relationships separate. But if he thought her idea was total crap, her pride was going to take a hit. And her feelings would probably be hurt.

"You'll do fine," Mrs. White said.

"Huh?" Carrie blinked, sure she'd heard her wrong.

"You're smart and the entire team respects you. You'll do fine."

Mrs. White was giving her a pep talk?

Coming from her, that actually made Carrie feel much better. "I have a lot riding on this."

"Well, no matter what happens in there, it won't change the way Rob feels about you."

Carrie opened her mouth to deny that they had anything but a professional relationship, then realized, by Mrs. White's wry smile, it would be a waste of time. Instead she sighed and said, "I hope not."

"I've known Rob almost his entire life. I've never seen him like this before."

"Like what?"

"Happy. Focused on something other than work."

"Mrs. White," she started, wanting to say something nice to the woman, but she shooed Carrie away.

"Go. He's waiting."

Carrie walked down the hall to the conference room. Mrs. White wasn't the only one who noticed a change in Rob. Tony, whom Carrie saw quite often now that he was dating Alice, had said basically the same thing.

"He's a different person when he's with you," he'd told Carrie, and she could only assume he meant that it was a good thing. It seemed to Carrie that Rob was happy, but with no frame of reference it was hard to know exactly how happy he really was now compared to before her arrival. She couldn't really ask anyone else, because no one else knew about them, so she was constantly second-guessing herself. Believing that things with her and Rob were so good, they were *too* good, and even if they ever did start to talk long term—which they hadn't—the relationship was bound to fail.

Maybe Alice was right. Maybe she *was* afraid to be happy. The question was, how did she stop being afraid? How did she learn to trust her own feelings, when deep down they were telling her that he was the one?

She stopped in front of the conference room door, took a deep breath, squared her shoulders and walked in. She'd expected the entire team to be there, but it was just Rob.

"Hey," she said. "Where is everyone?"

Her report was on the desk in front of him. "I wanted to talk, just the two of us first."

Uh-oh. That couldn't be good.

He gestured to the chair across the table from him. "Have a seat."

"You think it's crap, don't you?" she said, sliding into

a chair, feeling a bit like she was facing a one-man firing squad.

"On the contrary," he said. "I think it's brilliant."

She blinked. "Really?"

"And I'll show you why." From under her report he pulled a second report and slid it across the table to her. It was dated almost six months ago.

"What is this?" she asked.

"The report we put together before they made the decision to hire you. Take a look."

She flipped it open, noticing immediately how similar it was to hers—which wasn't too unexpected—but when she got to the proposed solution, her jaw dropped. "Oh, crap."

Rob laughed. "Yeah."

"Why didn't you show me this before?"

"Because you're the marketing genius."

She wasn't the only one. Rob and his team had drawn the same conclusions that she had, and with a few slight variations, the outline of his proposed plan was identical to hers. "Did you show them this?"

"They shot it down," he said. "Told me it was too radical. That we should stick to tradition."

It was radical because that was what the company needed to divert a potential disaster. Tradition was nice in theory, but to survive in the current economy, one had to change with the times.

No wonder Rob had been so resistant to hiring her. He'd come up with a plan himself that he knew was exactly what the company needed, but they hadn't trusted his judgment.

"They were wrong," she said.

"I know."

So they had just paid a tremendous fee to have her tell them what they had already been told. She could just imagine how well that was going to go over. What it would do to her reputation.

She dropped her head in her hands. "Oh, my God, I am so screwed."

"Why? You did exactly what they asked you to do. It's not your fault if they're too stubborn to listen to their own people."

"What are we going to do?"

"Work up a very detailed plan to present to them. Maybe this time they will listen."

"And if they don't? If they reject it again?"

He shrugged. "I'll resign."

She blinked. "You would really do that?"

"They're my family, and I love them, but that only goes so far. This is business. Family or not, how long would you stay on a sinking ship before you decided to jump?"

He was right. "So we'll give them the report and hope for the best."

The conference room door opened and Carrie expected to see Al, Will and Grant, but it was Nick who walked in.

"Sorry to interrupt. Have you got a minute?"

"Sure," Rob said. "What's up?"

"The news is going to spread fast, so I wanted to be the one to tell you."

"Tell me what?" Rob asked.

"Terri is pregnant."

At first Rob looked surprised, then he laughed and said, "Congratulations!"

He got up and walked around the table to shake Nick's hand, then gave him one of those man-hug things.

"I know how badly you guys wanted this," Rob said.

"We've actually known for about a month, but Terri wanted to wait to make sure everything was okay. You can't even imagine how tough that was."

"And is it?" Rob asked. "All okay, I mean."

"She feels great. The baby is growing exactly how it's supposed to. She's due September twenty-first."

"She's excited?"

"You would think she was the first woman in history to conceive a child."

Rob shook his head and laughed. "You and Terri. Who would have imagined?"

Nick grinned. "I know, right? Best move I ever made. I guess it was just our time."

Nick looked so happy, and Terri was lucky to have someone who loved her so unconditionally, Carrie actually felt a tug of jealousy. She'd always just assumed that some day she would settle down, get married and have a family, but only because that's what people were supposed to do. Now she realized it was something she wanted. *Really* wanted.

Al, Will and Grant walked in, and Nick told them the good news. There were more handshakes, hugs and congratulations, and she couldn't help feeling a little left out. Caroselli Chocolate really was like a big family. One she wished she could be a part of.

Rob looked over at her and grinned. She tried to imagine what it would be like, her staying in Chicago and moving in with Rob. Her and Rob getting married. Making their own excited announcement that she was pregnant...

Speaking of, she thought, trying to recall the date of her last period. Shouldn't she be starting soon? She'd been so busy lately that she hadn't even thought about it.

She picked up her phone and opened her calendar. Her last period had been not too long before she and Rob began officially dating, which was...

Her heart gave a quick squeeze. *Six weeks ago.*

No, that couldn't be right. It couldn't have been that

long. Because that would mean she was two weeks late. And she was *never* late.

She looked over at Rob. He must have sensed something was wrong. He was watching her with a furrowed brow.

She closed her eyes. This was not happening. It couldn't be. She could not be pregnant. She had been working her butt off and the stress was getting to her, that was all. Didn't Terri mention that stress could throw off a woman's cycle? Even though as long as Carrie had lived it had *never* happened before.

"Carrie?"

She looked up to find Rob standing beside her chair.

He leaned down beside her and lowered his voice, so no one else would hear him. "Are you okay? You're white as a sheet."

She couldn't draw enough air into her lungs to answer him, so she shook her head instead.

"What's wrong?"

Should she find out for sure first or tell him now? She hated to freak him out until he had something to be genuinely freaked out about. But was that really fair? And did she really want to do this alone?

"We need to talk," she managed to squeak out.

"Now?"

"Yes, now."

"Let's go to my office."

She rose from her chair, her knees squishy and her head spinning, hoping she would actually make it to his office. She had never passed out in her life, but it sure felt like she might now. He must have been thinking the same thing because he took her elbow to steady her.

"Where are you two going?" Al asked.

"Carrie isn't feeling well," Rob said. "Let's postpone the meeting until later this afternoon."

"Is there anything I can do?" Al asked, and hearing the concern in her voice, everyone else turned to them.

"It's not a big deal," Carrie lied. "I skipped breakfast. My blood sugar is just a little low."

"I'll take care of her," Rob told them, walking her to the door.

She wavered a little on the way to his office, but they made it there. She must have looked way worse than she realized because when Mrs. White saw her, she rose from her chair and said, "What's wrong?"

"She's not feeling well," Rob said as they walked past her desk. "Could you hold all my calls? And get us a cold bottled water from the break room?"

"Right away," she said, scurrying out.

Rob got her seated in his chair and sat on the edge of his desk. "Are you all right?"

She nodded. The initial shock seemed to be wearing off and she didn't feel nearly so woozy. "Sorry about that."

"How late are you?" he asked.

She was so stunned by the question that for a full thirty seconds she could barely breathe much less speak. "How did you…"

"I pay attention."

"To my menstrual cycle?"

"Not specifically. But when Nick announced that Terri was pregnant, it got me to thinking—"

"Thinking what?"

"That maybe, someday, that could be us. And then for some reason it dawned on me that since we've been dating I don't recall your having had a period. Then I looked over at you and you were pale as a ghost and checking your phone. Like I said, I pay attention."

"I can't be," she said. "There's no way I'm pregnant."

"Why not?"

"Because I just…*can't be*, that's why. I'm a little late, that's all. A measly two weeks. Stress can do that."

"It can?"

"That's what Terri said. Besides, we've been super-careful, right?"

"Well…" he said, trailing off.

"Rob?"

"We did have a small breach."

Her heart slammed the wall of her chest. "A *small* breach?"

"Very small, just a little tear."

"When?"

"A month ago, give or take."

"And you didn't *tell* me?"

"It didn't seem like that big of a deal. And I was worried you might freak out. Which I should point out, you are. I figured, there was nothing we could do at that point anyway, so there was no use worrying about it until we needed to. I was so not worried that until today, I forgot all about it."

"I can't have a baby."

She heard a throat clear and they both looked up to see Mrs. White standing in the doorway with Carrie's bottled water.

"Thank you," Rob said, taking it from her.

"Is there anything else I can do?" she asked, wearing what could almost pass for a look of sympathy.

"No. But please, just…keep this to yourself."

"Carrie?" Mrs. White said. "Do you need anything?"

Feeling shell-shocked, she shook her head. "No, but thank you."

She left, closing the door behind her.

"Actually, there is something you need," Rob said. "A pregnancy test."

Fifteen

"I don't need a pregnancy test," Carrie said, opening her water and taking a swig. Some of the color had returned to her skin.

"Would you rather see a doctor instead?" Rob asked her.

"I don't need either, because I'm not pregnant."

"And you know that because?"

"Because I *can't* be. That's why. I'm not ready."

"I don't think it works that way," he said.

"Besides a missed period, what other symptoms do I have? I don't have morning sickness and I haven't been especially tired. I feel completely fine. Totally normal."

"Maybe it's too early in the pregnancy for that."

"I am *not* pregnant."

"Wouldn't you like to know for sure?"

"I do know."

Her sudden descent into total denial was a little disturbing. "Carrie…"

"Just humor me, okay? Let's give it another couple of days. If I haven't started by then, I'll take a test. I just… I'm not ready to know yet. I need a few days to process this. And if I am, well, then I am. A few more days isn't going to make any difference."

He wanted to argue, because although she may not have wanted to know, he did. But shy of forcing her to take it, there wasn't a whole lot he could do. She was obviously scared and confused and pushing her would only make it worse. And she was right. If she really was pregnant, waiting a few days wasn't going to make a big difference. And there was no reason why he couldn't start making plans now, just in case.

"We'll give it until Monday," he said. "If you haven't started by then, we'll get the test."

"Sounds fair," she said. "If you don't mind, I think I'm going to go home early today."

"Go ahead. I'll stop by after work."

"Actually, I promised Alice we would do something together tonight. Maybe you and I can do something tomorrow?"

"Sure," he said. There was hardly a night they didn't spend together. Was it just coincidence that she chose today to spend the night away from him?

She probably just needed time to think.

She pushed herself up from his chair and seemed much steadier on her feet this time.

"Would you like me to walk you to your car?"

"No, I'll be fine."

"You'll call me if anything happens?"

"You'll be the first to know."

He leaned in to kiss her, aiming for her mouth, but she turned her head at the last minute and he got her cheek instead.

"I'll see you tomorrow," she said, offering him a weak smile as she walked out the door.

When she was gone, Rob sat down at his desk, feeling uneasy. Carrie's total lack of enthusiasm at the idea of being pregnant worried him. What if she really didn't want the baby?

There was a soft knock, then Mrs. White poked her head in. "Are you okay?"

"Yeah, I think so. A little…stunned, I guess." Or something like it.

"Are you sure there isn't anything I can do for you?"

"Any words of wisdom you care to impart?"

She considered that for a minute, then said, "A baby is a blessing."

"That's it?"

She smiled. "You don't need me to tell you what to do."

No, he didn't. With her time here running short, he'd already been seriously considering asking Carrie to relocate to Chicago. No, not just considering it, but he wanted to wait until the right time. When he felt she was ready to hear it. He knew that rushing things could potentially backfire. And he was more than willing to take things slow. The way he'd figured it, she could keep renting Terri's place, and in the appropriate amount of time, when they were both ready, move into his place.

It surprised him to realize that he was in no way disturbed by the idea of moving up his timetable. His feelings for her weren't going to change. And if he was going to collect his fifteen million, marriage would have to be part of the deal, anyway. He hadn't expected it to happen quite so soon, but he was ready. But how did Carrie feel? What if she wasn't ready?

She just needed time to process it, to get used to the idea of being a mother. Right now she was just scared. They hadn't actually discussed how he felt about their having a baby. Maybe she was worried that he wouldn't step up. Although he would hope she knew him better than that by now. But wasn't she used to people letting her down? He needed to assure her that he was behind this one hundred percent. That they would make it work. And in the process, he would earn himself a hefty chunk of change. Though he couldn't deny that the idea of profiting from the situation was a little...sleazy.

There was another knock on his door, but this time it was Nick who stuck his head in. "Hey, can I come in?"

"Sure."

He stepped inside and closed the door. "Is everything okay? I saw Carrie leave. You guys have a fight or something?"

"Not exactly."

"In other words, you don't want to talk about it."

Well, if anyone could understand what he was feeling, it would be Nick.

"Why did you turn down the money?" he asked.

"The baby money?"

"Yeah. You were married and planning to have a kid, anyway. Why not wait it out in case you did have a boy? I mean, where's the harm in that?"

"Because the money didn't matter anymore."

"Didn't matter how?"

"When it happens to you, you'll know." He paused as the light bulb suddenly clicked on. "Is Carrie...?"

"Maybe. Probably. But keep that to yourself."

"You know I will."

Rob shook his head. "This is surreal."

"Are you going to marry her?"

"Of course."

"If it's a boy, will you take the money?"

He shrugged. "That's what I don't know."

"Do you love her?"

"I've sure never met anyone like her."

"But is that a good enough reason to marry her?"

"You know that *Nonno* said we have to be married."

"Oh, so you want the baby, but you're marrying her for the money?"

No, but it sort of sounded that way, didn't it? And it wasn't like that at all.

"I'm going to marry her, because I *want* to marry her."

"You think she'll ever believe that when she finds out you took the fifteen million dollars?"

"How will she find out? No one but us knows about it."

"A lie by omission is still a lie, Robby. Is that something you could live with for the rest of your life?"

"Probably." Maybe.

"Until the answer to that question is hell no, you have no business marrying her. And you sure as hell don't love her."

The words stung, but even worse, Nick was right. As many times as he'd heard her say that he deserved better than her, she sure as hell deserved better than that.

Carrie called in sick the next day—leaving a message with Mrs. White—and wouldn't answer his phone calls all morning. When he got ahold of her after lunch, she claimed that she'd shut her phone off and had been sleeping. "I must have that bug that's going around."

"Can I bring you anything?" he'd asked.

"I don't want you to catch this. Anything I need Alice can get me."

"I take it we don't know for sure yet."

"If you're asking did I start my period, no, I didn't."

"Maybe under the circumstances you should go to the doctor, if you're sick and pregnant—"

"It's a bug, Rob. I'll be fine. I just need rest."

"I'll call and check in on you later, and if you need anything, call."

"I will."

She didn't call him, and when he tried to call her later that evening to check on her, it went straight to voice mail.

The next morning she called in sick again—Mrs. White took the call—and when he tried to call her back, she didn't answer. She texted him a little while later to say that she would be fine and to text if he needed her. It didn't take a genius to figure out that she was hiding from him, and he knew the best thing to do was to give her space. Give her time to deal with the idea of being pregnant. But by Monday, when he hadn't heard a word from her, voice or text, he reached the end of his patience. He left the office at noon and drove to her condo, with a quick stop at the pharmacy in between.

She opened her front door—and thank God she did open it—wearing orange sweat pants, a stained white sweatshirt and green slippers. Her hair, which looked as if it had gone days without seeing a brush, was pulled back in a limp ponytail.

He couldn't tell if she was sick, depressed or a combination of the two.

"Come on in," she said, looking equal parts guilty and apologetic. "I'm sorry I haven't called. I know that if there actually is a baby, that it's your baby, too, and I didn't mean to shut you out. I just didn't want to be that insipid, clingy woman who couldn't deal with things on her own."

"Carrie, you are the least clingy woman I've ever met."

"I'm the opposite. When things get too hard, I bail. You might want to keep that in mind, seeing as how I'm the potential mother of your child. What if I am pregnant, and we have the baby, and I bail on you both?"

"You won't."

"How do you know that?"

"Because I do."

"How?"

"Because you're a hell of a lot stronger than you give yourself credit for." He held up the bag. "We said Monday. So let's find out."

"And if I am?"

"We'll figure it out. Together."

She took a deep breath and held out her hand. "Let's have it."

He handed her the bag.

She gestured down the hall. "You want to watch me pee on a stick?"

"Do you want me there?"

"Why not? If we're going to do this together, we should do all of it together. Even this part."

For the past five days he'd been pretty confident that Carrie was pregnant, and the test was just a formality. But as he followed her to her bathroom, a ball of nerves coiled in his gut. If she was pregnant, his entire life was going to change. It stunned him to realize that as scary as that was, he was okay with it. Maybe he really was ready. Maybe, more than being nervous, he was just…excited.

He sat on the edge of the tub while she went through the process, which was pretty simple. Pee, then wait five minutes.

It was the longest five minutes of his life.

"Ever done this before?" Carrie asked.

"Once, in college. How about you?"

"Never." She rubbed her palms together. "So I'm pretty freaked out right now."

"In this case, practice does not make perfect." He looked

at his watch and his heart started to beat faster. "It's been five minutes."

"Here we go." After a slight pause Carrie very cautiously turned the stick over and peeked at the tiny display. She put it back down and exhaled, turning to him. "Negative."

He was so prepared to hear positive that when she turned and said negative instead, he was sure he misheard her.

"Negative?" he repeated, just to be sure.

She nodded, looking relieved. "I'm not pregnant."

"Oh." He wasn't sure what to say. "I really thought you were."

"But this is good news, right? I mean, you must be just as relieved as I am."

"You would think so." So why didn't he feel relieved?

"Rob, you are relieved, right? I mean, think about it. Sleepless nights, diaper rash, spit-up. College funds."

"I thought about it. And no, I'm actually not relieved. I mean, I know the timing wasn't great, but I'm still a little disappointed."

"Oh, thank God," Carrie said, holding up the test so he could see it. "Because I lied. It's positive."

"You *lied?*" Rob said, looking at Carrie as if he wasn't sure what to believe. "Why would you do that?"

"Sorry, but I had to know."

He took the test from her and checked it, then he shook his head, like he thought she was nuts.

He was probably right.

"You needed to know what?"

"How you really felt."

"You could have just asked me?"

"No. It's that nice guy syndrome."

"Nice guy syndrome?"

"You're a nice guy…a stand-up guy. So if I told you the test was positive you would have said you were happy, even if you weren't. Right?"

He hesitated.

"The honest truth."

"Probably," he admitted.

"But if you were disappointed that it was negative, even a tiny bit, then I would know that you were okay with it."

"That was risky."

She shrugged. "It worked on *Friends*."

"Friends?" He laughed. "You stole the idea from a *sitcom?*"

"Yup."

"Out of curiosity, what if I had been relieved? What would you do then?"

Good question. "I hadn't actually thought that far ahead. But at least I would know how you *really* felt."

"Tell me what you need from me," he said.

"How about a hug?"

Rob reached for her. She walked into his arms and he held her close, and she had the feeling that everything would be okay. She wasn't nearly as freaked out as she thought she would be. Maybe she was less freaked about the actual pregnancy, and more afraid of Rob's reaction. Not that she wasn't still terrified.

"What if I'm a terrible mother?"

"Think about it. If you learned nothing else from your mom and stepdad, it was how *not* to be a bad parent."

He had a point. Whatever they had done, she could just do the opposite. "What if I get scared and I bail?"

"I won't let you get very far."

"Really? Because I can be a very difficult person."

"Really. And you won't ever have to bail if you remember to communicate. If you just talk to me, I promise I'll listen. And whatever it is, we'll fix it."

It sounded wonderful, like a dream relationship. He also made it sound awfully easy.

But what did she know? Maybe for normal people it *was* that easy. Maybe if she was lucky, some of Rob's normal would rub off on her. Or maybe it was time she grew up and found her own normal. And stopped blaming all of her shortcomings on her crappy past. At some point she had to just let it go.

She could be anything she wanted to be. "It may take some time but I'll learn. Just try to be patient with me."

"I will."

She closed her eyes, nestling up against his chest. "Five days away from you is way too long."

He squeezed her. "I was thinking the same thing."

She breathed in his aftershave. It was so familiar now. *He* was so familiar. Suddenly *wanting* him was starting to feel a lot more like *needing* him.

"So what do we do now?"

Grinning down at her, he said, "I guess we have a baby."

Sixteen

Five seconds after he learned that Carrie really was pregnant, before he'd even had time to process it, Rob finally understood what Nick had meant the other day. It was one thing to think you might have a child, but to know it? There were no words. He and Carrie had a real shot at being a family. She could be the love of his life. Would he really jeopardize that for money?

Maybe *Nonno* was trying to do more than bribe them into having families. Maybe he was trying to teach them a lesson, too. Of what was and wasn't important in life.

He and Carrie agreed not to say anything to anyone until she'd seen a doctor. And there were still all these unanswered questions. Like where would they live? And would they get married? Carrie wondered how she would work and take care of a baby. Would she have to quit, or was it socially acceptable to put kids in day care?

And shouldn't they have at least a vague idea of what

they planned to do before they started telling everyone? Before people started asking questions they didn't have the answers to? And of course after the questions would come all the unsolicited advice.

So, the day the doctor gave them final confirmation, Rob knew they had to have a plan. And first things first. As soon as they got back to his place, he dropped to one knee and asked her to marry him. It wasn't as romantic as he'd hoped, but effective, because after asking him three times if he was really sure, she said yes. They decided that until they were married they would stay in their own places, but they would start looking for a bigger place that was a bit more kid-friendly than his loft, and unlike the condo, something with a fenced backyard. There was no mention of the L-word from either of them, but that was something he was sure they would both get to later. He didn't see any hurry, as long as they were on the same page.

After all of that planning, they decided to announce their marketing plan first. So no one could accuse her of being biased.

With everyone from the first meeting there, plus the entire marketing department, the conference room table was filled to capacity. "Well, let's have it," Rob's dad said, and Al passed out the folders.

It didn't take too long for the grumbling to begin.

"I'm getting old, son, but my memory is still pretty good," his dad told him. "Which is how I know that besides a few variations, this is the same plan you proposed last year."

"It's not." He gestured to Al to pass out the second set of binders. Personally, he didn't see the need to be so dramatic, but Carrie insisted that everyone see the difference between the two proposals. "This is mine."

"The first was mine," Carrie said. "And I did it with no knowledge of the first plan."

"Which means what?" Uncle Tony asked her.

"It means that I'm not the only marketing genius in the room. And I'm sorry, gentlemen, but you've wasted your money on me. Rob doesn't need me or anyone else to tell him what's good for this business. And you would all be fools not to listen to him. I know some of the ideas are a bit radical, and it's always nice when you can stick to tradition, but to survive in business, you also have to learn to change with the times."

His dad steepled his hands, looking to his brothers, then finally to Rob. "Well, son, it would seem we owe you an apology. We should have trusted you, listened to what you had to say. But we didn't and we paid the price."

"And now?" Rob said.

"I want to see a combined report on my desk by Wednesday."

"We anticipated that as a possibility," he said. "Al, number three."

Al passed out the third round of binders.

"Here's your combined report."

"Give us a day to look these over, and we'll meet again Thursday."

As everyone was piling out of the room, Rob pulled his dad aside.

"While you're feeling so forgiving, there's something I need to tell you." Carrie cringed a little as he gestured her over. Rob slid his arm around her shoulders and pulled her close to his side. "I'm not sure if you know, but Carrie and I have been seeing each other. Socially."

"Should I act surprised?"

Meaning he—and Rob would bet a lot of other people in the family—already knew they were a couple.

"Well, Carrie is pregnant."

"Okay," his dad said. "*Now* I'm surprised." He looked back and forth between the two of them. "I don't like that I have to ask this, but can you both assure me this had nothing to do with the proposal you just presented us?"

"He didn't show me his until I showed him mine," Carrie said, then cringed when it sank in what she had just said. "That did not come out right."

"I understand what you meant," his dad said. "And don't worry, you'll fit into the family just fine. Assuming that's the plan."

"She's staying in Chicago, we're getting married, we're going to buy a kid-friendly house or condo and we are going to put the kids in day care because even though we love them to death, we both love our jobs and neither of us wants to give them up."

"When is the baby due?"

"Around Halloween," Carrie said. Which they both found a little creepy considering the basement door and cradle incidents.

Since the day they'd brought the cradle up to the living room, the door stopped opening by itself. The cradle hadn't rocked again either. At least, not as far as he, Carrie or Alice had seen. It was almost as if someone or something knew they were going to be needing it.

It was creepy, yet comforting in a strange way to know that whatever it was, it had their back.

Within twenty-four hours, everyone in the family *knew* Rob's dad was going to be a *nonno,* and then his mother made sure everyone knew it was actually Rob's baby that would give him the title, because no one was clear on that point.

Everything was falling into place, almost too smoothly,

but there was one more thing that he had to do. He called *Nonno* and told him he didn't want the money.

"I'm proud of you" was all *Nonno* said, as if that was the reaction he'd been expecting all along. And while giving up fifteen million wasn't too tough, Rob wondered if Tony would be able to resist the draw of the entire thirty million for himself.

After Mrs. White left for lunch, Nick poked his head into Rob's office. "So you're really going to do it?"

"Do what?"

Nick leaned in the doorway. "Tie the knot, have a baby. It's worth the fifteen million?"

"You're forgetting I don't get a penny if it's not a boy."

Easygoing as Nick was, it took a lot to rile him. Now he was riled. "You're seriously going to take the money?"

"What reason do I have not to?"

"Dude, *seriously?* Where should I start?"

"How about, I love her. That would be a good reason."

Nick narrowed his eyes at him. "Are you screwing with me?"

Yeah, and it was awfully fun. "I called *Nonno* and told him no deal. I'm not taking the money."

"When?"

"A little while ago. You were right. No amount of money is worth screwing this up. I can live without the money, but I can't live without her."

"What did *Nonno* say to you?"

"That he was proud of me."

"He said the same thing to me. I got the distinct feeling that he counted on us not taking the money. Like that was part of the plan."

"That might not work with Tony." While Nick and Rob both loved the satisfaction of doing their job well, Tony lived by the philosophy that he who dies with the most toys wins.

"I guess we'll just have to wait and see," Nick said. "He seems pretty smitten with Alice, and it looks as though the feeling is mutual."

Rob shrugged. "Maybe *Nonno* will actually manage to get us all married off before this year is over."

"And there's a fifty-fifty chance that one of our kids will be a boy."

So there was hope that the Caroselli name would live on for at least one more generation. Rob also didn't doubt for a second that even if there had been no baby, no accidental pregnancy, they would have eventually wound up in the same place.

A half hour or so after Nick left, Rob got a call from Alice of all people. And for some reason she was whispering.

"What the hell happened? Did you and Carrie have a fight?"

A fight? "No, why would you think that?"

"Because she's packing."

"Packing what?"

"Her *stuff.* She's shoving it all into suitcases. She's *furious.* If she knew I was talking to you right now she would kill me."

"I haven't talked to her since this morning and everything was fine then." Could it just be cold feet? "Did she say anything?"

"I tried to talk to her, but she wouldn't say what was wrong. All she said was that she was going back to L.A. *Alone.* She said I could stay at the condo until the lease ran out."

This sounded like something a bit more serious than cold feet. "Don't let her go anywhere," he told Alice. "I'll be there as fast as I can."

Seventeen

Rob made it to Carrie's condo just as she was shoving her bags into the back of her SUV. He parked in the driveway behind her, so she couldn't make a run for it.

He climbed out of his car and said, "Going somewhere?"

"Home," she said, shoving the last bag in, not even looking at him.

"You are home."

"Home to L.A."

"Can I ask why?"

"If you can't figure that out for yourself, you're an even bigger ass than I thought."

"What the hell happened?" She started to walk away and he reached for her arm.

She spun to face him, yanking it free. "Don't touch me. You don't ever get to touch me again."

She wasn't just a little upset or even scared. She was

seething mad. She stomped into the house and he followed her.

"Carrie, I honestly have no idea what's going on."

She spun around to face him. "Fifteen million dollars, Rob. Fifteen million to get married and have a male heir. Is this ringing a bell?"

Oh, crap. "You heard me and Nick talking."

"Did you knock me up on purpose, or was it just a happy coincidence? And is this the real reason why you were disappointed when I said it was negative? Why you didn't ask me to marry you until after I saw the doctor?"

"It wasn't like that. If you had heard our entire conversation you would know that."

"Did your grandfather offer you fifteen million dollars to get married and have a male heir?"

"No one is supposed to know about that, but yes, he did. What you heard was me screwing with Nick. I wasn't planning to take the money. I had already called *Nonno* and said I didn't want it. If you had stayed and listened you would have heard me say that I can live without the money, but I couldn't live without you."

"Sure you did."

"You don't trust me."

"After what you did? How could I possibly?"

"I don't mean now. You never did. If you trusted me you would have come to me first. You would have stuck to the plan. We would have talked about this, figured it out together. Like you promised. But it's so much easier to bail, isn't it?"

"That's not what I'm doing," she said, but she didn't sound quite as confident anymore.

"No, that's exactly what you're doing. It's all you know how to do. I thought that because I really love you, it would be different for us. But it's not, is it? It never will be. No matter what I do to prove how much I love you, it will never be enough. I'm going to spend the rest of my life chasing you, because running is all you know how to do."

"Haven't I told you a million times that you deserve better than me?" she said.

"You did. And shame on me for not listening. Have your lawyer call my lawyer and we'll work out some sort of custody arrangement," Rob said, then turned and walked out the door.

Carrie wasn't surprised, and still, she felt sick. Sick all the way through to her soul. He'd given her all sorts of chances, put up with more crap from her than the average guy ever would, and once again she'd gone and screwed it up. She had driven him away, when what she should have done was tell him that she loved him, too, and that she was just scared. The sad part was that she really did believe that he wasn't going to take the money, but it had been the perfect excuse to drive him away. Because he was right. That was all she knew how to do. If she had stuck to the plan and had just talked to him, they could have worked it out. Everything would be fine now. They would be making wedding plans, and looking for a place to live.

And as much as she wanted to race after him and beg him for another chance, tell him she would do anything to make this right, she didn't deserve another chance.

She'd hurt him enough.

She closed her eyes and took a deep breath, but it did nothing to quell the feeling of panic swirling inside her. The realization that she loved him. Really truly loved him. And maybe she didn't deserve another chance, but she wanted one. If she could just convince him that this time it would be different, that she would never doubt him again. If she could catch him before he drove away...

She opened her eyes and nearly jumped out of her skin when she realized that he was standing right in front of her. For a second she thought that she had conjured him up out of her imagination. Until he shook a finger at her and said, "You almost had me."

"I did?"

"I made it all the way to my car before realizing what an idiot I am. I accused you of not sticking to the plan, but I did the same damn thing."

"You did?"

"I told you that if you tried to bail on me, I wouldn't let you get far. You needed me to prove that I'll be there, that I'll fight for us. Instead, I bailed on you. So this is where I draw the line. This is as far as I let you go."

"Okay."

He blinked. "Okay?"

"Yes, because you're absolutely right. I was looking for a reason to push you away, but only because I am absolutely terrified by the idea that you might actually love me. But you know what? I love you, and being afraid and in love sure beats being all alone."

"From this day forward, for better or worse, like it or not, you are stuck with me."

Even after all that, as he held his arms out to her, it took every bit of courage she possessed to walk into them. To take that final step, that last leap of faith. But she did it, and she knew without a doubt, as they wrapped their arms around one another, neither would ever let go again.

* * * * *

REQUEST YOUR FREE BOOKS!

2 FREE NOVELS PLUS 2 FREE GIFTS!

HARLEQUIN *Desire*

ALWAYS POWERFUL, PASSIONATE AND PROVOCATIVE

YES! Please send me 2 FREE Harlequin Desire® novels and my 2 FREE gifts (gifts are worth about $10). After receiving them, if I don't wish to receive any more books, I can return the shipping statement marked "cancel." If I don't cancel, I will receive 6 brand-new novels every month and be billed just $4.30 per book in the U.S. or $4.99 per book in Canada. That's a savings of at least 14% off the cover price! It's quite a bargain! Shipping and handling is just 50¢ per book in the U.S. and 75¢ per book in Canada.* I understand that accepting the 2 free books and gifts places me under no obligation to buy anything. I can always return a shipment and cancel at any time. Even if I never buy another book, the two free books and gifts are mine to keep forever.

225/326 HDN FVP7

Name	(PLEASE PRINT)	
Address		Apt. #
City	State/Prov.	Zip/Postal Code

Signature (if under 18, a parent or guardian must sign)

Mail to the **Harlequin® Reader Service:**

IN U.S.A.: P.O. Box 1867, Buffalo, NY 14240-1867
IN CANADA: P.O. Box 609, Fort Erie, Ontario L2A 5X3

Want to try two free books from another line?
Call 1-800-873-8635 or visit www.ReaderService.com.

* Terms and prices subject to change without notice. Prices do not include applicable taxes. Sales tax applicable in N.Y. Canadian residents will be charged applicable taxes. Offer not valid in Quebec. This offer is limited to one order per household. Not valid for current subscribers to Harlequin Desire books. All orders subject to credit approval. Credit or debit balances in a customer's account(s) may be offset by any other outstanding balance owed by or to the customer. Please allow 4 to 6 weeks for delivery. Offer available while quantities last.

Your Privacy—The Harlequin® Reader Service is committed to protecting your privacy. Our Privacy Policy is available online at www.ReaderService.com or upon request from the Harlequin Reader Service.

We make a portion of our mailing list available to reputable third parties that offer products we believe may interest you. If you prefer that we not exchange your name with third parties, or if you wish to clarify or modify your communication preferences, please visit us at www.ReaderService.com/consumerschoice or write to us at Harlequin Reader Service Preference Service, P.O. Box 9062, Buffalo, NY 14269. Include your complete name and address.

SPECIAL EXCERPT FROM

 HARLEQUIN

Desire

Olivia Gates

presents

TEMPORARILY HIS PRINCESS

Available May 2013 from Harlequin® Desire!

Vincenzo Arsenio D'Agostino stared at his king and reached the only logical conclusion.

The man had lost his mind.

Ferruccio Selvaggio-D'Agostino—the bastard king, as his opponents called him—twisted his lips. "Do pick your jaw off the floor, Vincenzo. No, I'm *not* insane. Get. A. Wife. ASAP."

Dio. He'd said it again.

Mockery gleamed in Ferruccio's eyes. "I've needed you on this job for *years,* but that playboy image you've been cultivating is notorious. And that image won't cut it in the leagues I need you to play in now. When you're representing Castaldini, Vincenzo, I want the media to cover only your achievements on behalf of the kingdom."

Vincenzo shook his head in disbelief. "*Dio!* When did you become such a stick in the mud, Ferruccio?"

"If you mean when did I become an advocate for marriage and family life, where have you been the last four years? I'm the living, breathing ad for both. And it's time I did you the favor of shoving you onto that path."

"What path? The one to happily-ever-after? Don't you know that's a mirage most men pursue until they drop in defeat?"

Ferruccio went on, "You're pushing forty…"

"I'm thirty-eight!"

"…*and* you've been alone since your parents died two decades ago…"

"I have friends!"

"…*whom* you don't have time for and who don't have time for you." Ferruccio raised his hand, aborting his interjection. "Make a new family, Vincenzo. It's the best thing you can do for yourself, and incidentally, for the kingdom."

"Next you'll dictate the wife I should 'get.'"

"If you don't decide, I will." Ferruccio gave him his signature discussion-ending smile. "'Get a wife' wasn't a request. It's a royal decree."

But Vincenzo knew it wouldn't be that easy. Like his king, Vincenzo had been a one-woman man. Unlike his king, he'd blown his one-off shot on an illusion.

Even after six years, the memory of her sank its tentacles into his mind, making his muscles feel as if they'd snap….

A realization went off in his head like a solar flare.

A smile tugged at his lips, fueled by what he hadn't felt in six years. Excitement. Anticipation.

All he needed was enough leverage against Glory Monaghan to make his proposal an offer she couldn't refuse.

Will Glory say yes?

Find out in

TEMPORARILY HIS PRINCESS by Olivia Gates.

Available May 2013 from Harlequin® Desire
wherever books are sold!

HDEXPO413